# A CHANCE GONE BY

*Brides By Chance*
*Regency Adventures*
*Book Two*

## Elizabeth Bailey

SAPERE
BOOKS

# A CHANCE GONE BY

Published by Sapere Books.

20 Windermere Drive, Leeds, England, LS17 7UZ,
United Kingdom

saperebooks.com

ISBN: 978-1-912786-55-8

# Chapter One

Even with the double doors open to the vestibule and the staircase beyond, it was insufferably hot. Added to the press of brightly-clad guests shifting under two massive chandeliers, with the windows tightly closed against the harsh March winds, there was a distinct lack of air.

Marianne Timperley plied her fan vigorously, aware that her discomfort was not wholly attributable to the prevailing atmosphere in the stuffy ballroom. Her pulse was behaving in an irregular fashion, becoming more unruly as she scanned each new set of arrivals, and she did not see the face she had nerved herself to confront with every appearance of normality.

She was conscious of the fact that she had begged the family not to be made to stand with them in the receiving line. Especially when the son of the house, Justin Crail, officially Lord Purford since the death of his father, who should have been here at the start to take his place, chose to be disgracefully late.

Rowsham's announcement heralded another set of guests and Marianne's heartbeat quickened briefly and subsided again when she took in the new faces. No Justin yet.

This suspense was playing havoc with her self-control. While she curtsied in her turn and murmured a greeting, digging into the fog of her mind for a couple of innocuous remarks, Marianne began to think of leaving her post. Imprisoned in this fashion, her customary good sense had vanished. She could better employ her time and energy in making a discreet check that all her careful arrangements were in place and everything was running smoothly.

Taking advantage of a lull in the stream of arrivals, she whispered to Jocasta at her side: "Surely nearly everyone is here now? I might slip away."

Her cousin's expressive young countenance, lively with a mixture of excitement and apprehension, turned towards her. "Don't desert me, Marianne, I beg of you. You promised!"

That was undeniable. Indeed, it was owing to Jocasta's insistence that she was standing here at all. With an inward sigh, Marianne pushed her own troubles away, and tried for a note of reassurance. "Yes, I did. It's just so hot."

"Hot? I'm shivering with fright!"

Marianne conjured a smile. "You look delightful and it's your ball. I told you, all that is required of you is to enjoy yourself."

"And behave demurely, and not shock all the starchy matrons, and —"

"Jocasta, be quiet!"

The hissing admonition came from Grace, Lady Purford, resplendent in a robe of crimson-coloured sarcenet trimmed with black lace, her neck and ears bejewelled, her dark locks bedecked with a white and crimson feathered head-dress. Her attitude was only too clear a justification for poor Jocasta's fears. In vain had Marianne tried to hint to her cousin Grace that her daughter would do better at her come-out if she were not plagued with a catalogue of restrictive rules.

"I will not have her taken for an impertinent hoyden by the likes of Lady Burloyne and the Marchioness of Colgrave. And that wretch Mrs Guineaford, who thinks herself so high merely because a coterie of foolish men is convulsed by her wit, would be all too glad of an excuse to take me down."

Marianne interpreted this without difficulty, being fully acquainted with the rivalry subsisting between her cousin Grace and the peerless Mrs Guineaford. The latter's success arose more, she suspected, from her immense wealth than her dubious reputation for uttering *bon mots*.

"Dear ma'am, it is highly unlikely Mrs Guineaford will expend one moment's energy on Jocasta. I doubt she will even notice her. As for attending the ball —"

"That is just what I am saying, Marianne. She will attend, if only to spite me, and be on the watch to jump the instant Jocasta says one little thing out of place, which you know she is bound to do. It is all Justin's fault! He has spoilt her to death and see what has come of it. She is totally unfitted to be let loose in company and I will be blamed."

Recognising the futility of argument once the refrain of Justin's mishandling of his half-sister had entered the lists, Marianne had applied herself instead to reassurance.

"Recollect, ma'am, there will be three of us to keep an eye on Jocasta. Unless you mean to turn off Miss Stubbings now that she no longer needs a governess?"

"Certainly not. The child has every need of the woman, for I cannot be forever at her side once we are established in Town, and I will have more need of you than Jocasta. It is the greatest comfort to me, Marianne, with my uncertain health that I can depend upon you. But all that is beside the point. I will not have my daughter considered too free and if I must drum it into her head from morning to night, then so be it."

And drum she did, Marianne reflected, recalling how often poor Jocasta had run to her in floods, declaring she'd rather remain a spinster than be subjected to the frightful ordeal of becoming a debutante. As for the prospect of her presentation to the Queen, she had claimed to be in a regular quake months before the event.

Between soothing Jocasta's tears and, later, listening with what patience she could muster to Grace's complaints and dire prophecies, Marianne had had her hands full in the lead up to Jocasta's coming out ball. Once preparations for departure to London had begun, she was burdened in addition with the many domestic crises plaguing the housekeeper and butler. Rowsham's austere requests were easier to deal with than Mrs Woofferton's prognostications of disaster, which were almost as dismal as those of her mistress, although pertaining to the inadequacies of the female servants rather than those of Lady Jocasta Crail.

It was as well she had been too occupied to chafe at Justin's long absence and worry at its meaning. Just as she had done all last year, on tenterhooks every time he left the estate.

The crash had come upon her in a wholly unexpected fashion three weeks into the season when she was preoccupied with organising the ball — which could not be delayed once Jocasta's long-dreaded debut had at last occurred at the Queen's February drawing room — as well as dealing with the escalating panic of all concerned. She had come late into the dining parlour where the other three ladies were already seated at the reduced dining table, an innovation Marianne instituted to give the place a cosier feel in the mornings. She had been delayed by a tearful Nancy, who had endured a scold for clattering the fire irons in the grate and waking the dragon Stubbings far too early.

"You've missed Justin," Grace had announced, setting down her cup and reaching for one of the pile of fresh spiced buns in a silver dish.

Marianne's heart had done the little flip it always did at the mention of his name. But she kept her voice even as she crossed to the side table where the butler was waiting to serve her from the several covered dishes set out there. "Is he back at last? Did he come to breakfast?"

"Breakfast? No! He rushed in and out so that we barely had time to take it in."

Jocasta, her mouth full of spiced bun, chimed in. "Would you believe it? He has finally offered for Lady Selina."

The shock had been severe. Marianne felt her mind go blank and spots began to dance in her vision, but she had pulled herself together. She waved away the proffered viands and contented herself with a couple of oat cakes. Busying herself with buttering them and spooning blackberry jam on to her plate had afforded an excuse not to meet anyone's eyes.

"To tell you the truth," Grace had said as she stirred her coffee, "I had quite given up hope of his fulfilling Sessay's expectations. It was an understood thing for years between him and my dear lamented Purford."

"Yes, and last year he never came up to scratch, though he danced attendance on her all through the season."

Miss Stubbings, severe in purple chintz, looked up from her plate, where she was addressing a substantial breakfast of baked eggs and ham, and bent her spectacles upon her charge, tutting in a reproving way. Grace immediately took it up.

"Jocasta! That is precisely the sort of remark…"

"But it's only us, Mama. There's no one to hear me."

Miss Stubbings cut in, stiff with disapproval. "Besides, how do you know that, Lady Jocasta? You were not out and therefore not present to observe it."

"Oh, Delia wrote to tell me, for she made her debut then, and if you ask me, she was hoping to attach Justin herself, only she never quite said so or I would have warned her that he was pretty well promised."

"Jocasta!"

"Gossip, Lady Jocasta, is the work of the devil. If I have told you once, I have told you fifty times."

Marianne did not hear much of the ensuing peal rung over her cousin's hapless head by her mother and preceptress. It had been as much as she could do to preserve her countenance and hold back the tide of misery threatening to engulf her. Long practice came to her rescue. Schooling her features, she maintained a spurious air of calm, passing off her lack of appetite on disturbed sleep. Not that she could flatter herself any of the combatants noticed.

She would have been glad enough to escape to her room, but there were far too many calls upon her time to allow for that indulgence, which had proved useful, since the common activities of the day served to buffer the shock and dull the pain. At least until the night hours, when sleeplessness really had claimed her, though by then she could not weep, which might have afforded some relief.

Instead she had tossed and turned, berating herself for allowing that tiny seed of hope to fester. She'd long known the futility of her impossible dreams. Justin was not for her, never had been.

Yet she'd hugged their close friendship to her heart, believing it compensated for the more intimate relationship. Only a traitor streak of obstinacy had snaked its way into her bosom, declaring that it might be, it could be — if only Justin loved her. It would take that, if he was to defy convention, defy his commitment to his deceased father's arrangement, and ignore Marianne's utter ineligibility as the potential wife of an earl. He could not and would not choose his stepmother's poor relation, orphaned daughter of an obscure naval lieutenant.

Even if he loved her as desperately as she loved him. Which he did not. He did not love her at all. Except as a friend. If one could call it love when he had been carelessly kind and obliging to an unhappy girl, in whom he learned to confide. But everyone did that, did they not? It meant no more than simple trust and an ease of confidence that Marianne would not betray him. Naturally she would not. She would die first.

But he had not confided in her when it came to the question of his marriage to Lady Selina Wilkhaven, most eligible daughter of the Earl and Countess of Sessay. He had hesitated all last year, causing Marianne to suffer a series of aching questions as to his intentions. Indeed, she hardly saw him, even during the rare times he was at home. When they met, he was as indulgent towards her as ever, but Marianne sensed distance between them, which she'd put down to her own disturbed condition.

Marianne's racing thoughts were interrupted and she was abruptly brought back to the present.

"Forgive me, dear Grace, but it truly was not my fault."

The light, caressing tones jerked Marianne's pulse into high gear and she had all to do to remain standing. Her legs turned to jelly and she had to grip her fingers together to stop their trembling. He was here. He had come at last.

"There was an unfortunate accident just as we were setting out, and my poor Selina was obliged to change her dress. You are acquainted with Lady Selina, of course, ma'am."

Marianne heard Grace's reply through a haze as she took in the radiant vision at Justin's side. Lush dark curling locks, a creamy complexion, sweeping lashes over eyes as blue as the sky and the face of a fairy princess. How could she possibly compete?

"Jocasta, my charming girl, you look delightful."

His sister preened, turning this way and that to show off the elegant spotted silver muslin drapery that adorned her short-sleeved white gown, fixed to the front and shoulders with Wedgwood medallions. A double row of pearls was clasped about her neck and a gold medallion decorated the large curl at the front of her hair, the rest caught up in ringlets.

"Do you think it pretty?"

"Indeed I do. If I shower you with compliments, will you forgive my tardiness?"

Justin bowed over Jocasta's hand in the teasing fashion he invariably used towards her, the customary glint in his eye.

"Never, you heartless wretch!" Jocasta declared, at once falling into her normal spirited self instead of the demure pose she'd perforce been wearing.

"Alas! What shall I do to make it up to you?"

"I'll think of something, be sure. But at least you are here to lead me into the first dance."

Justin threw up hands of mock horror. "Good God, does that fate await me?"

"Horrid creature! You know it does. And I won't tread on your toes. I've been practising."

"I am relieved. Though I've no doubt you'll find some way to unhorse me and I'll crash to the floor and embarrass us all."

His sister's giggles unfortunately attracted her mother's attention.

"Jocasta! For heaven's sake, Justin, don't encourage her!"

Marianne saw the siblings exchange a conspiratorial glance of understanding and then Justin was before her, his smile crinkling the corners of his eyes in the way she loved.

"Marianne."

Her name on his lips set the seal on her despair. Her heart was drumming in her chest and she had difficulty finding her voice. She put out her hand, and his touch as he took it seared her fingers even through the glove.

"You're shockingly late," she managed, trying to speak normally through lips that felt stiff and alien.

"But with very good reason," he returned, releasing her and drawing his companion forward. "Allow me to present Lady Selina Wilkhaven. Our cousin, Miss Timperley."

Marianne dropped a curtsy, dredging up a smile. "May I offer you my…" The word 'sincere' stopped her tongue. Heavens, what in the world was she to say? "…my warmest congratulations?"

"Thank you. Most kind."

Selina had a delightful mellow voice, as well as everything else. No one would suppose she'd had to change, for she looked stunning in a white gown embroidered in gold and trimmed with fur, ornamented at the sleeves with diamond loops that matched the diamanté in her hair and around her throat. She turned away immediately.

"Do we remain with your family, Justin? Or should we join the throng?"

*Join the throng, please*, Marianne begged silently, unnerved by the thought of having to stand alongside the creature who had dashed her future to pieces. Herself modestly attired in a blue-spotted Russia robe over a plain gown, her hair mostly concealed by a *chiffonet* of light blue satin with silk-trimmed ends and a single feather, Marianne knew she would be completely outshone.

Fortunately, Grace intervened. "We will all go on, I think. Now that Justin is here, we may shortly start the dancing. Marianne?"

"I will see the musicians, ma'am."

"Find Miss Stubbings, if you please, and send her to me."

"As you wish, cousin."

Thankfully moving away, her limbs still unsteady, she heard Grace behind her. "You had best circulate, Justin, until the dancing begins. Jocasta, stay by me until he comes to claim you. Or if I should be occupied, Miss Stubbings will be here directly."

Glad of the necessity to resume her duties, Marianne tried to ignore the deadness in her chest as she pinned a rictus smile to her lips.

# Chapter Two

Leaving his betrothed surrounded by her usual court, Justin went in search of his sister, prepared to hear a more comprehensive complaint than Jocasta would dare with her mother's ears flapping beside her. If Grace would only let the child be, she would do very well. Nothing could more surely prejudice her chances than stifling her natural vivacity and presenting her as just one more colourless debutante.

Though he doubted, with an inward chuckle, that Jocasta's exuberance would remain buried for long. Once she found her feet and was permitted to be out of the Dragon's or Grace's sight for more than five minutes, Justin had no doubt she would revert rapidly into the pert and bubbly enchantress who had long since learned how to twist him around her little finger.

At least their dance would afford her an opportunity to show her true colours. He would be at pains to provoke her. He owed her that much, after appearing so disastrously late.

His irritation revived. He could scarcely blame Selina for tripping over that urchin, who dashed across the path just as she was about to enter his carriage. Justin was only too aware that his own inattention had been responsible for her fall. Worse, he'd gone directly to pick up the ragged boy and set him on his feet before attending to his fiancée.

Her wrath was perfectly justified, and he should have apologised immediately, instead of giving in to annoyance. He had lifted her to her feet and seen the damage at once. Her cloak was awry and a swathe of darkness against the pale material of the gown all down one side told its own tale.

"Dear God, your dress is wrecked! I suppose that means you must change it?"

Selina had pulled the cloak aside in order to inspect her skirts, but at that she raised her head, the fine eyes blazing. "Do you expect me to appear at your sister's ball in this?"

"No, of course I don't."

The words were automatic, but Justin inwardly seethed at the delay as he helped her up the steps. The front door of the Sessay town house was still open, and Justin found the butler at his elbow.

"I will summon her ladyship's maid, my lord."

Selina had spoken up, her tone sharp. "Tell my parents also, Moffat. No doubt my father will entertain Lord Purford while he is waiting, and Mama will assist me."

What, was he to chafe under his prospective father-in-law's eye while Selina dawdled her way into a fresh gown for another couple of hours or more? She'd already made them late.

"I will do better to go home now and return for you later on, don't you think?"

Selina had halted on her way to the stairs and turned on him a face of fury. "So that you may leave me kicking my heels here while you forget all about me?"

He had glanced quickly around, but they were alone, the butler having gone upon his errands. "Don't be absurd. I'll be back in —"

"If you imagine I am going to make this first public appearance without your support, you are mightily mistaken, Justin."

"No such thing. I have every intention of coming back to fetch you."

Her eyes had glittered in the candlelight. "I am all too familiar with your dilatory intentions, I thank you. If there is one thing I may trust you to do, it is to keep me waiting."

He had been so angry he held himself from opening his mouth until he could command his voice.

Triumph showed in her face and she nodded. "Wait! I will not keep you above an hour."

Justin watched her cross to the stairs and climb steadily, her back rigid. His spurt of fury devolved into the weight of depression already becoming familiar. That her taunt was justified served only to add to the resentment which had held him back so long from acting on the expectations of all parties concerned.

How neatly had his father tied his hands! He'd been obliged to hold off any involvement with an eligible female until Selina came out last year. Justin had paid court to her throughout the season. If he must marry her, at least let them become better acquainted. When Selina's beauty rapidly acquired for her a large circle of male admirers, Justin indulged the hope her affections might be drawn elsewhere. It did not happen.

She had reserved her warmest smiles for Justin. Lady Sessay dropped broad hints, and her lord began to look at Justin askance. Several times he'd been on the brink of asking for an interview with Lord Sessay and found himself unable to carry through. At the season's end, both Lord and Lady Sessay had made their disappointment clear.

"Well, Purford, and have you sown enough wild oats yet?"

He'd been able to turn that one off easily enough, but Lady Sessay proved a deal more embarrassing.

"I confess I had not expected my lovely girl to reach the end of the season unbetrothed, my dear Purford. So many rivals for her hand, you know. But she's a good, dutiful girl, who would never wish to disappoint her parents."

That had been said with a significant look which he could not mistake. He'd returned some answer, but he'd known his doom was sealed. There could be no escape.

Nevertheless, he had held off, throwing himself into a frenzy of social activity and spending as much time as he could spare from the management of his estates away from Purford Park. Whether he was indulging in an orgy of final freedom or only trying to school himself into forgetfulness, Justin did not know. A little of both perhaps.

But with Christmas over and the new season looming ahead of him, he knew he could no longer put off the inevitable. No announcement came to provide him with a last minute reprieve. He had posted north and put his fate on the line.

The Sessays, at once relieved and delighted, had invited him to remain, with the expressed justification that it would give Selina and her newly betrothed time alone before they must face the *ton* together. Justin managed to delay the announcement for the three weeks he spent with the family.

"It would be grossly uncivil in me to allow it to become public before I had informed Lady Purford and my sister."

Lord Sessay had accepted this, but his lady had given him a look which clearly stated that if he thought the delay might afford him an escape, he would soon learn his error.

But Justin, having resigned himself, had set out to charm and woo his future wife. His efforts met with little success. She was ice-cold and brittle, and he began to suspect she had accepted him with as much reluctance as he had proposed. Until she made it obvious she was punishing him.

18

"You do realise you made me a laughing stock last year?"

The remark had come out of the blue. They had been out riding and had reined in after a gallop. Selina patted her horse's neck and turned to look at him.

Justin was so much taken aback by the suddenness of the attack he had been lost for words for a moment. "Then I must beg your pardon," he said lightly at last.

Selina's gaze was steady. "Yes, you must."

He frowned. "If I offended you, Selina, I am truly sorry."

"You didn't offend me. You subjected me to the mockery of the *ton*. That is hard to forgive."

He stared at her. "Mockery? When you were more courted and petted than any other female?"

Her eyes snapped at him. "Oh, pray don't let us continue this farce!"

"Farce? What in the world —?"

"If we are to make any sort of a life together, Justin, we cannot go on pretending."

"Would you care to be more specific?"

Bitterness had sounded in her voice. "This match between us was arranged years ago. Neither of us had any choice in the matter, I imagine."

Justin had been conscious of a measure of relief, but he was hurt too. "That may be true, but you will allow I gave you ample opportunity to choose another, if you are so averse from my suit."

She looked away, biting her lip. He had watched her, wondering if there was here a chance for relief. For her as well as himself, if she was truly against the match. He was glad the announcement had not yet been made.

"Selina, if you truly don't wish to marry me — if there is someone else perhaps, then —"

She looked at him then, her eyes hard. "There is no one. And of course I wish to marry you. Did I not show myself willing enough all through the season?"

"Willing? Can we not try to make it more than that, Selina?"

"When you have made it abundantly clear that you don't really want to marry me?"

He had been shocked to realise how much he must have given away, and knew not how to contradict her without sounding insincere.

"You need not look like that, Justin. Let us admit that neither of us would have chosen the other if it had been possible to choose, and be done."

"Is that it? Is that all the effort you are prepared to make?"

To disappointment had been added dismay and a burgeoning anger. Had he sacrificed his feelings for this?

Selina urged her horse into a walk and he perforce followed suit.

"You will not find me wanting, Justin. I know my duty."

"Duty? If that is to be the sum of it, Selina, let me set you free. We are not obliged to follow the dictates of our respective parents, you know. We do not live in the Middle Ages."

At that, she had uttered a spurt of laughter. It had sounded hollow to Justin's ears.

"True, but I'm afraid there is no going back now." She looked at him, a little smile wavering on her lips. "Besides, I have never said I was unwilling. It is an excellent match, after all, and I could scarcely wish for a more personable husband."

"I thank you," he said drily.

"I am persuaded we will deal well together... in due course."

Justin was less sanguine, but he did not say so. He had agreed to it and the subject was never brought up between them again. Selina unbent a trifle in her attitude towards him, and he hoped his lapse might be forgiven. But she was never warm, often spiky, and the slightest misstep or mishap seemed to afford her an excuse to prick at him.

After the accident with the carriage his prospective father-in-law had ushered him into the saloon to wait. Lord Sessay had come down the stairs not moments after his daughter went up them, tutting distressfully.

"An unfortunate accident, my dear boy, but Caroline has gone to expedite matters. I am persuaded all will be rectified swiftly. I have told Moffat to bring refreshments. You will take a glass, I hope?"

Justin had acquiesced perforce, removing his cloak and smoothing the superfine sleeves of his green coat, relieved his satin knee-breeches had not suffered the fate of Selina's gown. A quick glance in the mirror above the fireplace served to reassure him that the fracas had not disarranged his intricately tied cravat. He touched the diamond pin to set it again and turned to accept a glass of wine from his host, whose insouciant manner revived his irritation.

"Never does to arrive too early at one of these affairs, after all. Only have to endure the tedium for a good deal longer than necessary."

Justin had refrained from retorting that the entertainment was his sister's debut ball, and he was expected to be there to greet the guests. Lord Sessay would consider his first duty was to his betrothed, which he supposed it now was. Jocasta would be disappointed, but he could more easily deflect her upset than deal with Selina's megrims. His little sister adored him and he cared for her a great deal. That made all the difference.

Justin's thoughts faded and he turned his attention back to the present as he caught sight of Jocasta standing demurely at her mother's side, conversing with one of Grace's matronly friends, although there were several young gentlemen hovering discreetly nearby. Her dance card would fill up rapidly once he led the way.

Suppressing his personal concerns, Justin moved in to interrupt, summoning every ounce of the vanished air of gaiety his sister both deserved and expected.

Jocasta was soon chattering in her usual animated fashion every time they came together in the dance. He listened with half an ear as his brooding thoughts intruded once again, until she shocked him out of his inattention.

"She is very lovely, but I truly didn't think you'd do it, Justin. I always supposed you and Marianne would make a match of it."

# Chapter Three

While she passed among the guests, exchanging a smile here and a word there, Marianne could not stop her gaze straying to the set where Justin was now dancing with his betrothed.

He had done his duty by his sister, who did not lack for partners. She went from one dance to the next, with insufficient time between to return to Grace's side, thank heavens! Instead, her friend Delia Burloyne waylaid her, with another couple of females in tow. An excellent turn. The more young ladies she became acquainted with, the less she would be shadowed by her mother. And the Dragon had disappeared, probably in the direction of the card room.

Relieved, Marianne did not trouble to keep more than a cursory eye on her cousin, which unfortunately left her with the far less arduous duty of ensuring the guests were well entertained. After more than four years of deputising for Grace, this was second nature. While she questioned and responded, therefore, she could not school her attention to refrain from drifting.

Had she been asked, she could have said at any moment exactly where Justin was in the room. His fair head, his well-remembered smile and the easy grace of his movements obtruded all too easily into her line of sight.

An unwelcome voice cut into her attention.

"So he's popped the question at last."

Marianne turned to confront the gaunt figure of Justin's paternal aunt. A tall woman with the characteristic Crail hawk nose in a long face — attributes Lord Purford had thankfully not bequeathed to his son — Lady Luthrie had come to

Purford Park at Christmas with her husband, bringing also her son and her newly married younger daughter whose spouse was on foreign shores with his regiment. She had not hesitated to speak her mind at length on Justin's failure to fulfil his father's expectations, driving even Grace into the snappish resentment that afflicted everyone else.

"She is very beautiful," Marianne said, unwilling to hear more of the evident satisfaction in Lady Luthrie's tone.

"Beautiful, well brought up and eligible in every way. My brother knew what he was doing. When is the wedding?"

Marianne flinched inwardly. "I have no notion, ma'am. We only learned of the engagement a bare day before the notice came out."

The elder lady humphed, the ornate feathers on her turban nodding in sympathy. "I will advise Grace to urge an early date. We don't want him crying off."

Instinct sent Marianne flying to Justin's defence, but she managed to maintain her customary cool tone. "He won't do that. He is too much the gentleman."

"He was not too much the gentleman to keep the girl waiting for the better part of a year," came the acid response.

Marianne kept her lips firmly closed, but her eyes followed Lady Luthrie's glance and she allowed herself to dwell on Selina's elegant figure performing the movements of the dance with practised ease.

"Well, let us hope for the best." Lady Luthrie turned back to Marianne, brows raised. "And what will you do, my dear, when Grace retires to the Dower House? Go with her? I doubt she could manage without you."

Shock held every faculty suspended for a moment as Marianne stared into the woman's face. Her expression was not unkind, but the blunt question thrust reality into play, killing the dream stone dead.

Marianne would no longer run Justin's household. She must give up the reins, pass them across to the woman who had already taken the one thing that mattered to Marianne above all else. It had not before occurred to her that she would lose the rest as well.

"I don't know, ma'am. I have not had time to think about it."

"Well, I dare say there is no rush. Grace must get Jocasta off her hands before she can think of retiring from Purford Park. But I would advise you, Marianne, to look to your own future. You are young yet, you present a good appearance and I am bound to state you have all the qualities needed to be the wife of a sensible man."

An exasperated laugh escaped Marianne. "I thank you, Lady Luthrie, but I fear there is one lack which cannot be overcome."

"Fortune? Nonsense. There are gentlemen enough who can afford to take a dowerless wife." Her fan swept an arc as if to encompass these gentry. "You cannot hope to marry high, but a sound investment in a man of sense will secure you."

"An investment? I had not thought of it in that light, I confess."

"Because you were never brought out in the usual way, my dear. Nor had you a careful mama to think of these things. However, it is not too late. If you will be guided by me, you will look about you for a widower in search of a stepmother for his children. Such men are far less particular."

Despite the pain it caused her to think of spending her life with any other man than Justin, Marianne found it hard to contain her bubbling amusement. "My dear ma'am, I am not acquainted with any widowers — other than our neighbour, who is sixty if he is a day. But if you will point me in the direction of any such fellow, I will at once set my cap at him."

Lady Luthrie's look of approval very nearly overset her altogether. "I will give it some thought." She tutted. "Really, Grace has been remiss. She might have got you off years ago if she hadn't chosen instead to lay her burdens on your shoulders."

Marianne opened her mouth to refute this, but Lady Luthrie set a hand on her arm, bending the strong nose in her direction.

"No, do not defend her. You have borne your trials cheerfully, and I admire you for that, Marianne."

"Ma'am, you mistake. Anything I do in the house, I have taken upon myself. Cousin Grace is not to be blamed."

The elder lady pursed her lips. "That does not excuse her leaving your interests out of her calculations. Had I been consulted, I would have recommended Grace to set her snare for the Reverend Underwood."

"But he's married."

"He wasn't when he took up office. He would have been ideal for you, had Grace bestirred herself and not allowed him to be snatched up from under her nose."

Marianne was prevented from expressing her relief that her cousin had refrained from foisting her on to the local vicar by the entrance of a new voice into the discussion.

"What is this, Aunt Pippa? Are you scheming to get poor Jocasta riveted before she has had time to enjoy Society?"

Her amusement quenched, Marianne had all to do to keep her countenance as the rhythm of her pulse speeded up and her throat constricted. She was glad to hear Lady Luthrie take up the gauntlet.

"No such thing, my dear Justin. As to your sister, I anticipate no difficulty. She will take."

"What, even with the faults you were enumerating at Christmas?"

His aunt's fan waved this aside. "Nothing that cannot be speedily nipped in the bud. No, it is Marianne's future I am thinking of."

Marianne saw the startled look in Justin's face with a rush of dismay. She dared say he had never given the matter a thought.

His eyes turned on her, those magnetic eyes whose unusual green colour had fascinated her from the first. The old teasing gleam entered them.

"Have you caught the matrimonial fever then, Marianne?"

She found her voice, trying for a like insouciant tone. "No, indeed. The notion came out of your aunt's head, not mine."

"It ought to have done," said Lady Luthrie, thrusting her intimidating beak towards Justin. "Everyone has been preoccupied with securing your engagement — the dearest wish of your father's heart, I may add —"

"Yes, I am aware."

"Not to mention Jocasta's come-out," continued her ladyship, ignoring the snapped interjection, "but this should have been thought of. It's not your business, dear boy, to be finding a husband for Marianne, but I am minded to tell Grace just what I think of her."

Justin's smile of practised charm appeared, the one he used to smooth his way out of any potential argument. "I must beg you will hold off, Aunt Pippa. Grace is so much agitated with what she conceives to be the difficulties in getting Jocasta off, it would be unkind to burden her with another worry."

"That, ma'am, is all too true," Marianne cut in. She had no desire to enter into a series of fruitless discussions on a subject that must prick her with too many pins to be bearable. "And to tell you the truth, I have far too much on my hands at this moment to be able to pursue the matter myself."

Lady Luthrie's lips pursed but she evidently saw the force of these arguments, for she gave a decisive nod, and the feathers fluttered. "Let it be so for the moment. But it will not do to be forgetting it altogether, Justin. Once you bring your bride home, Marianne's position will be invidious, to say the least."

With these measured words, she moved on, leaving Marianne confronting Justin, who was regarding her with a good deal of concern.

"I had not considered it, but she's right, Marianne. Selina will expect to take over the household. Not immediately, but in due course."

"Naturally." She hoped her smile concealed how ill-at-ease she felt, though her pulse had steadied a little. "I will accompany Grace to the Dower House, although I suspect she will not wish to make the move until Jocasta is married."

"Nor would I expect it of her. Or you, Marianne. Hang it, Aunt Pippa is in the right of it! You should have been provided for. I ought to have —"

"Pray don't get into one of your fusses, Justin," she interrupted, a streak of irritation rising. "I am — I have been — perfectly content. I never expected to marry and I don't intend to start repining now."

"I know that, but it does not excuse us. I see now that we have taken unfair advantage of you, and…"

"Justin, if you must harp on about this, pray don't do so in the middle of Jocasta's ball. You should rather be attending to your betrothed."

"She is dancing with someone else at this moment. And for the Lord's sake don't say I should be hovering about Jocasta, driving the poor girl mad."

"Your guests, then. You are the host, little though anyone might think it, considering your late arrival."

His face changed. "That was not my fault."

She raised her brows. "Indeed? Are you being towed around by the nose now?"

The flash in his eyes warned her, but Marianne paid no heed. It was easier to be angry with him than to endure the agony of knowing he was lost to her.

"That was uncalled for."

"Was it? Well, it seems to me that someone needs to remind you of your duty."

His eyes narrowed. "I'm well aware of my duty, I thank you."

"Then go to it!"

His lips tightened, those lips she had so often dreamed of feeling against her own. They parted, and his voice came out clipped. "We'll finish this at a more appropriate time."

# Chapter Four

Lying wakeful in the darkness of her curtained bed, Marianne tried in vain to halt her tumbling thoughts. Uppermost was remorse for wasting her brief moments in Justin's company. Their last exchange was typical of the others they'd had this last year. Why could they not meet without snapping at one another? What had happened to the ease of friendship?

Well, on her side there was no difficulty in finding the cause. Ensconced at Purford Park with no means of observing for herself, she'd been on tenterhooks for the imminent news of his betrothal. During his few visits home, she had lost all the natural ease they'd previously enjoyed. Justin must have felt it and been puzzled. Hurt perhaps?

No, for he'd been too preoccupied to be thinking of the disintegration of their friendship. Which was inevitable, now she came to look at it. How could he maintain a close — not to say intimate, though there had been nothing for either to be ashamed of — relationship once he was married to someone else?

Not that Marianne had ever truly believed she had a chance, despite the dreams. Deep down she'd known, even as she approached marriageable age, her case was hopeless. Knowing it had not prevented her from wishing, even from scheming. She remembered how naively she had planned how Justin would crown her day on her eighteenth birthday with the longed-for offer. She remembered too, with a downward sweep at her stomach, how she had toyed with the notion of proposing herself when he did not.

She had actually opened her mouth to say the words, but her courage had failed her. Not so much because it was not done for females to make the approach. More because she could not persuade herself that Justin loved her. He was as fond of her as he could be, that much she knew. But was his affection of the kind that led to marriage?

She had not known and fatally, had hesitated. Naturally she had saved herself a world of embarrassment when she learned soon after that Justin was virtually promised to Lady Selina Wilkhaven, who was not yet old enough to wed him.

Months passed before she recovered from the severity of disappointment and despair. If she had not found occupation in making herself useful, Marianne knew she'd been in danger of turning into one of these die-away melancholy heroines in the novels devoured by Grace. When her cousin's eyesight began to deteriorate, Marianne had taken to reading to her and was, in consequence, all too well acquainted with the sort of green melancholy that afflicted these fictitious creatures. A salutary lesson. She had determined never to wear her heart on her sleeve.

She had succeeded so well that not even Jocasta knew the secrets of her bosom, though she had once or twice remarked upon her brother and Marianne's obvious liking for one another, which was genuine. Just when her fondness for him had deepened into love, she was unable to say. She could not remember a time when her affections had not been engaged. She had adored Justin from the day his innate kindness had made him befriend the gawky twelve-year-old he'd found huddled on the bench of the old oak tree, weeping out her loneliness.

What would you? When a tall, blond and handsome prince leapt off his horse to the rescue, was any youthful maiden to be blamed for feeling as if she had stepped into a fairy tale?

He was seventeen or eighteen then, not much more than a callow youth, but to Marianne's eyes he was all a hero should be and more. He had comforted her tears, made her laugh, and on discovering her identity, hailed her for his cousin. Not that they were in truth in any way related.

Which was why he'd understood. Marianne remembered, with a surge of feeling, how he had been the first person to refrain from telling her she must be strong.

"It's hell to lose your mother. And you've lost your father, too," he'd said bluntly. "You're entitled to cry as much as you need."

The permission immediately made it possible for her to bear her double loss with fortitude. One of the things she loved in Justin was that he never tried to varnish the truth. He was always forthright. Just as he had last evening taken up the matter of her future the instant it was pointed out to him.

Marianne sighed, realising her thoughts had come full circle and she was nowhere nearer sleep.

She must have dropped off at last, for she woke heavy-eyed when Nancy drew back her curtains and presented her with her morning cup of chocolate, the one luxury she allowed herself to indulge. Despite being treated kindly, she never forgot her dependent state and could not bear to take advantage of Justin's generosity, for it was, after all, he who footed the bills.

She found it easy enough to reject all but the most necessary accoutrements suitable to her situation, though it had taken ingenuity to persuade Grace away from providing her with a wardrobe almost as extensive as Jocasta's.

"I am not a girl in the first blush of youth, ma'am," Marianne had told her. "And I'm definitely not on the catch for a husband. I don't need to deck myself out like a debutante."

"I won't have you dressing like a governess, Marianne," had protested her benefactor. "If I am not up to it, you'll have to chaperon Jocasta, don't forget. You can't go about looking like a dowd."

Marianne had perforce accepted this dictum, but managed to curtail expenditure on herself by dint of dwelling on Jocasta's needs. Marianne's more modest acquisitions escaped Grace's notice. At least she was able to present an acceptable appearance upon those evenings when she had to roam in public. Unlike the unfortunate Dragon, who was not included in Grace's benevolence and had to be content to make a figure of herself in an old-fashioned gown of embroidered white taffeta too young for her years, or else choose a purple-coloured figured muslin that had seen better days.

It was odd how Grace could be amazingly generous and yet given to bouts of thoughtlessness, even to occasional spite. She had not the true spirit of aristocratic charity, finding the necessary role of lady bountiful towards the poorer tenants a penance to be endured rather than the compassionate duty of her state. She'd been visibly relieved when Marianne offered to be her deputy in such matters, which had undoubtedly contributed to Lady Luthrie's displeasure with her sister-in-law.

Contrary to that lady's belief, failing the dearest wish of her heart, Marianne was content to remain a spinster, and to continue to occupy the unofficial post of Grace's companion, which enabled her in some sort to repay her cousin for taking her in and giving her a home, one act of charity for which she'd earned Marianne's undying gratitude.

At least she would remain in Justin's vicinity. She would see him from time to time if she lived at the Dower House.

For the first time, she wondered if this was wise. Would a complete break not be better than seeing him in the clutches of his rightful wife? Should she perhaps consider his aunt's words with more care?

She finished her chocolate on the thought. It festered as she began to prepare herself to face the day.

# Chapter Five

The relief of being back in the family home affected Justin not a little. There was no need to be on his guard, to endure the platitudes of Selina's mother, the hearty encouragement of her father. Until he sat at breakfast in his own dining parlour in Hanover Square, with the day free before him, he had not realised how tense he had become.

He had been home yesterday, of course, but then the ordeal of public acknowledgement and congratulation was still before him and both Grace and Jocasta had been in the natural state of nerves to be expected before the ball. Marianne had not appeared at breakfast, and he had been out until it was time to change his dress ready to dine with the Sessays before escorting Selina to Jocasta's come-out. And a sorry farce that had turned out to be.

Recalling Marianne's sarcastic taunt, a resurgence of irritation cast a cloud over his better mood. Why did she cut at him like that? She must know his loyalties had shifted perforce. What choice had he when his betrothed must take precedence over his sister? And he had tried to come away.

Doubt seized him. Should he have forced the issue? Was he allowing the oppression of guilt to dictate his actions?

Before he could formulate a response to his own question, Marianne entered the dining room. Justin's breath tightened.

She checked on the threshold and her glance met his. "Oh, you're here before me."

"Yes, I didn't ride this morning."

She turned her gaze away and crossed to the sideboard, where Simon moved to assist her with the covered dishes there.

Justin's appetite deserted him and he laid down his knife and fork, abandoning the remaining slices of beef and ham. He took up his tankard, but one mouthful of ale was enough. "Coffee, Rowsham, if you please."

The butler picked up the silver pot and poured from it into his cup. Justin signed to him to remove the offending plate and sipped at the liquid. It was hot and appropriately bitter.

He watched Marianne pull back the skirts of her sprigged muslin gown in the way she always did to make herself comfortable, and take her seat in her usual place at the side of the table, a little removed from Justin at the head. He regarded her over the rim of the cup as she thanked Simon when he placed her plate with her chosen breakfast before her. She was eating lightly as usual. Justin doubted whether a baked egg and a couple of buns could sustain her through the day.

"You look a bit drawn, Marianne. Didn't you sleep well?"

She threw him a look, her brows knitting briefly. "Not wonderfully, no."

"In other words, you tossed half the night. Or what was left of it."

A faint echo of her warm smile flitted across her face and Justin's chest caved in. He spoke without thinking. "Marianne, don't be at outs with me."

At that, her eyes came up and that clear gaze flashed him a warning as she indicated the servants. Hell's teeth! He'd forgotten they were not alone. Urgency gripped him. He must speak to her in private. "I take it Grace and Jocasta are still abed?"

She had taken up a fork and was toying with the egg. She nodded without looking at him. "I don't imagine either will rise before noon."

Then this was his opportunity. "We'll serve ourselves, Rowsham. I'll ring if I need you."

He noted Marianne's frown as she watched the butler and footman leave. As the door closed, she turned a wary countenance towards him.

He did not hesitate. "I wanted to talk to you alone."

She grimaced, setting down her fork and reaching instead for her cup. "Yes, you said last night you were not finished. Are you going to try and persuade me into setting my cap at some unsuspecting victim?"

He winced inwardly. "No, I'm not." Involuntarily, he reached his hand towards her. "Marianne!"

She looked at it, but she did not respond as she used to do. Justin waited a moment, his spirits sinking, and then withdrew it. The hand felt awkward, like a spare limb he did not know what to do with. He curled it around his cup with the other and took refuge in his coffee.

Her rejection hurt him. He could see by the tightness in Marianne's face that she knew it. Didn't she care? He could not keep silent. "Is this how it is going to be?"

He heard her sigh.

"It has to be, Justin."

"But why? I've no better friend than you, Marianne. Or so I supposed."

She looked up and the ghost of a smile tore at him.

"You're going to be married. Don't you think your wife will look askance at any such intima— friendship, with another woman?"

He did not miss the slip. "Intimacy? It was never that. Selina can accuse me of nothing untoward."

She flushed. "I didn't mean — it was the wrong word. I know your fondness is of the brotherly kind."

Was it indeed? He could not express how his feeling for Marianne was very different from his affection for Jocasta. For one thing, he never had the impulse to confide his deepest secrets to his half-sister. Of course she was a good many years younger than Marianne. Too young to be able to enter into those matters that nearly concerned him.

"I've missed our ramblings, Marianne."

"I too."

Her voice was low and she did not look at him. He'd hurt her somehow, he was sure of it.

He tried again. "We talked together of everything under the sun. You used to confide in me."

She looked up and reached for her coffee. She was perfectly composed, or she seemed to be. "So too did you confide in me."

Justin was conscious of confusion. It was true he had not taken her into his confidence throughout the miserable months of hoping Selina would settle on another man, leaving him free to choose. How could he do so? He could not discuss it, even with so close a friend as Marianne. Especially with her. Did she resent his having held off?

"Marianne, this last year —"

"Don't, Justin." Her clear gaze caught and held his. He read a world of regret there, but determination too. "Nothing stays the same. Circumstances change things. We have been close, and you will always have a special place in my heart. But —"

He could not bear it. "Marianne, don't talk as if you meant to say goodbye. I know it can't be the same, or quite the same. But I can't lose you altogether. It's bad enough without —"

He clipped the words off short, horrified by what he had been about to say. Shock hit him as he realised Marianne had gauged the situation more nearly than he. Not even to Marianne could he declare the dread and dismay with which he regarded his coming nuptials. How could he speak of Selina at all without at once giving away his distaste and betraying the woman who must from now on command his trust?

Already he had said too much. Marianne was eyeing him with concern in the grey gaze. He tried to retrieve his error, improvising as best he could.

"I'm finding it difficult to … to cope with the necessary changes. I'm so used to Jocasta's liveliness and your common sense, and Grace's…" He hesitated and was grateful when Marianne laughed and helped him out.

"Grace's megrims and woes?"

He grinned, relaxing a little. "Just so."

"She doesn't mean to be selfish, you know."

"Yes, I know. She was always kind to *me*."

He had not meant to emphasise the last word. Grace was not precisely unkind to her cousin, merely inconsiderate. Marianne did not take it up.

"I'm sure it will be strange at first." She sounded encouraging, if careful. "For Lady Selina, too."

"Yes."

He could drum up no words to describe Selina's possible attitude towards the household. They would find out soon enough how prickly and difficult she could be.

"We will all do our best to make her welcome, Justin."

"I'm sure you will." He knew his tone was colourless, and tried to adjust it. "I know I can rely on you."

"You can indeed." She smiled. "I daresay Lady Selina may find it odd that I am so very much involved in the running of the house. But I will naturally hand over the management to her whenever she wishes it."

Justin could think of nothing to say to this. He had no notion how Selina would play it when she took up her position as Lady Purford. If he was to judge of their relationship so far, he could see only a crumbling disintegration into separate lives. A dismal prospect. He must make more of an effort and find a way to get her to respond to him.

He glanced at Marianne, who was pouring herself a refill from the coffee pot. Why could he not succeed with Selina as he did with Marianne? He had never had the slightest difficulty in cajoling or teasing her into the comfortable interaction they had enjoyed. Until now. It struck him she had become as unpredictable as his betrothed.

A stray thought caught at him. Was she jealous? No, impossible. She was unhappy at the lack of closeness — intimacy she'd almost called it. She could scarcely be jealous of Selina. She hardly knew her. Did she, like Selina, feel neglected?

The thought no sooner entered his mind than he gave it voice. "Marianne, have I neglected you? Is that why you are distant? Did you begin to think I no longer valued our friendship?"

Marianne was staring at him, her eyes wide, the coffee cup frozen by her lips. He could not read her expression and it was a moment before she answered. He watched her as she turned away and set down her cup in its saucer. Was she thinking how to reply? It occurred to him he was not going to get the truth.

When she looked at him again, the startle was gone from her eyes and the smile on her lips did not reach there. "Perhaps a little. We scarcely saw you for months. I did miss you. Though we were very busy preparing for Jocasta's come-out. I suppose … I suppose I felt the coming change." She smiled again, and the bleakness of it struck at Justin like the cold of winter. "Perhaps I've been trying to adjust."

Had not they all? But he could not say that. Instead he gave her the truth. "Never imagine, Marianne, that I don't value the closeness we share. If you ever need me — for anything at all — I am yours to command. You must know it."

Justin saw the tremble at her mouth, and, with a lurch in his chest, the moisture gathering in her eyes. Her voice, when she spoke, was husky.

"Thank you, Justin. I needed that."

Then she leapt from her chair and walked quickly out of the parlour, leaving him peculiarly bereft.

# Chapter Six

April had warmed up and Marianne seized the opportunity to get out of the house and blow her crotchets away with a brisk walk. Lately she'd been tied up sharing the task of chaperoning Jocasta since the Dragon had retired to bed with a sore throat which had developed into a full-blown cold. Never one to mince words, she'd told Marianne — the only member of the family permitted into her chamber — that she could not risk her charge taking it from her.

"I will not reappear until all possibility of infection is past. We cannot have the child falling ill. Dear Lady Purford has several delicate nudgings on hand and it could be fatal to interrupt them. Pray convey my apologies to their ladyships."

Marianne replied suitably, knowing Jocasta would jump for joy at the news. Not so Grace, who wavered between dread of catching the cold herself and bemoaning the lack of Miss Stubbings to keep Jocasta in line.

No one, thought Marianne wryly, worried that *she* might go down with the Dragon's cold. She was rarely ill, although so pulled at present she would not have been surprised if she succumbed.

As well she did not, since she had no time to spare to coddle herself. The chambermaid Nancy, detailed to wait upon the Dragon, took the cold from her, and conveyed it to the kitchen maid. As the harassed Mrs Woofferton confided to Marianne, to have two of her girls out of action and the rest of the servants' hall in danger was enough to send a lesser body into strong hysterics. Marianne directed her to hire a couple of temporary maids and privately asked Simon to take as much of the burden off the housemaid as he could.

"We can't have poor Ellen trudging up and down the stairs with hot water jugs as well as dusting the downstairs rooms before breakfast. And Mrs Woofferton won't ask you, I know, as she doesn't like to encroach upon Rowsham's domain."

Simon grinned. "Mr Rowsham has already given me the office to do downstairs, Miss Marianne, but I'll help Ellen carry the jugs too."

What with the domestic crisis and taking Jocasta about when Grace's strength failed her, Marianne should have been far too occupied to dwell on her own unhappiness. But the nagging ache returned whenever she had a spare moment and Justin was never far from her thoughts.

She saw little of him and could not decide whether it was a blessing or a curse. She would have to become accustomed since this was how it would be for the future. But her stubborn heart refused to obey the dictates of her mind. She missed him, and in the rare times she saw him, her consciousness in his presence prevented her from saying anything but the most commonplace remarks.

It came as a relief therefore to don her bronze pelisse and the new chip straw hat, and slip away with the excuse of going to change Grace's library books. She headed towards Old Bond Street, enjoying the fresh air and entered Hookham's Circulating Library with a lighter heart.

It was pleasant to browse the shelves, her eyes passing idly over titles she might like to read but knew would not appeal to Grace. She kept her eyes open for tales by Fanny Burney or Clara Reeve, while hankering rather for Swift or the amusement of Fielding.

She had just spotted *Camilla*, one of her cousin's favourites, when her eye was caught by a couple a few feet away. They were standing close enough to whisper and had chosen a discreet corner for their rendezvous.

Marianne must suppose it was a rendezvous for the man, dressed in the scarlet coat and white breeches of the military, had one hand clasped upon the female's upper arm and his head bent towards her as he talked in a fashion that looked particularly earnest. The woman had her back to Marianne, but by the cut of her blue spencer, the elegance of her gown and the frivolous beribboned bonnet, she was a lady of fashion.

As Marianne watched, she turned her head, presenting a lovely profile and a glimpse of dark hair.

A jolt of recognition went through Marianne. Lady Selina Wilkhaven!

Conjecture rattled through her mind as Marianne saw Justin's betrothed move to one side, changing her position sufficiently to be able to notice the attention. Their eyes met. Lady Selina's brows drew together briefly, and then cleared as she let out a gasp.

The instant of consternation was swiftly conquered. Lady Selina stepped away from her cavalier and moved to Marianne, holding out her hand.

"How do you do? You are a relative of Justin's, are you not?"

The mellow voice was matched by the graciousness Marianne had first encountered. Astonished by the woman's quick recover, she took the hand, trying for a like insouciance.

"His cousin." Realising that Lady Selina had forgotten her name, she supplied it. "I am Marianne Timperley. In truth, I am Lady Purford's cousin, but Justin is kind enough to include me in his family circle."

Lady Selina smiled, but Marianne thought she looked brittle.

"Ah, I understand." Selina gestured to her companion and he came forward. "You must allow me to present Colonel O'Donovan. Miss Timperley, Gregory."

Marianne noted the informality of her address to the man. Had the Christian name slipped out? The military gentleman bowed from his superior height. As Marianne dropped a curtsy, she decided he looked all too conscious. Was this an assignation? Lady Selina's next words showed she felt her situation called for explanation.

"Colonel O'Donovan is an old family friend from Yorkshire. I've been acquainted with him from childhood, you must know. Such a surprise to see him here."

The colonel spoke up. A deep voice, redolent with feeling. "I've been abroad, ma'am. My regiment was posted back to England only a short while ago. It was a … pleasant surprise to meet Selina — I mean Lady Selina — in this place."

He glanced, as he spoke, at the surrounding shelves, as if he had never seen them before. Suspicion deepened in Marianne's mind.

"You are fond of reading, colonel?"

He looked startled. "Why, yes. Though such opportunities are few."

"I imagine they might be." Marianne hoped her tone was not too dry. Lady Selina was eyeing her in a way that made her feel like a predatory snake. It became imperative to demonstrate disinterest. She smiled brightly. "I have come for my cousin Lady Purford. Her eyes are bad and she likes me to read to her."

"How kind," murmured Lady Selina, and a measure of relief seeped into her countenance. "Though I dare say it must be a tedious duty."

"I enjoy reading aloud. Besides, it is the least I can do."

Lady Selina's brows rose. "I understood you do a great deal more for Lady Purford."

What had Justin been saying about her? The notion he had mentioned her to Lady Selina was not welcome. Or was she doing him an injustice?

"Indeed? Did Justin tell you that?"

"No, I had it from his aunt."

"Lady Luthrie?"

"She is a friend of my mother's, you must know."

Worse and worse. God send that interfering busybody had not confided her plans for Marianne's future to this creature or her mother! She made haste to change the subject, turning to the colonel. He was not precisely handsome, but a trim moustache and a small scar running down the edge of his left cheek gave him a dashing air. Perhaps Lady Selina was not to be blamed if she was a trifle dazzled.

"Do you make a long stay, sir?"

He reddened. Now why?

"I hardly know. It depends. My plans are uncertain."

"Colonel O'Donovan is subject to the whim of the regiment," cut in Lady Selina, in so obvious an attempt to relieve him that Marianne's grew even more suspicious. "I hope to see a little more of him before he is whisked away."

"Your parents too, no doubt." There was no mistaking the alarm in the colonel's face. Marianne smiled. "A family friend, I thought you said?"

Lady Selina's answering smile became fixed, though it did not reach her eyes. "Just so." She inclined her head. "I must take my leave, or I shall be late for an engagement."

The colonel started. "Allow me to escort you as far as the carriage, ma'am."

"So kind, thank you. Goodbye, Miss Timperley."

Marianne returned her nod, dropped a curtsy to the colonel, who was bowing, and watched Lady Selina leave Hookham's, her hand demurely resting on the gentleman's arm.

All desire to find a book had left Marianne. She stared unseeingly at the shelves, her mind seething with question.

There was undoubtedly something between the two. That it was a chance meeting she did not believe for a moment. Both were far too conscious, though Lady Selina covered it better. Besides, their attitude before they had perceived her was far too intimate to suggest anything other than a pre-arranged meeting. The rhythm of her pulse speeded up with a ridiculous rise of hope. Which sank again almost immediately.

That this was a prior attachment was clear. Colonel O'Donovan might be a disappointed lover, might have only learned of the betrothal on his return, but he must have known about Lady Selina's expectations. That she returned his regard was evident, but it was equally apparent any proposed match between these two had been thwarted long before Justin offered.

Had the colonel been an acceptable parti, Lady Selina had ample time to persuade her parents into cancelling the arrangement made between the lords Sessay and Purford years ago. No, this was a dream as impossible as her own had been.

Pity rose in her, together with a spurt of rage at the insensitivity of both fathers. Why must four people be made unhappy merely for the sake of status? An earl's daughter to marry an earl? Yes, an excellent match in Society's eyes. But what a dreadful waste!

For if Lady Selina was in love with this Gregory O'Donovan, she could never make Justin happy. How sad to be obliged to marry against her heart. Sadder still to cause distress in the abandoned lover as well as the prospective, unsuspecting husband.

All thought of her own misery vanished in the abrupt realisation that Lady Selina must fear to be betrayed. She might well imagine Marianne would relay the encounter to Justin.

She was instantly beset with the vexed question of what she ought to do. Should she warn Justin? Was it fair to stay silent and allow him to marry Lady Selina when she was clearly in love with another? On the other hand, if Lady Selina had indeed given up her love on the altar of duty, what right had Marianne to interfere? Worse yet, was she reading more than was justified into a meeting that might be quite innocent?

With the couple no longer before her, doubt crept in. Had she made a false judgement? Even had they met by design, it could well betoken nothing more than a nostalgic moment alone. Perhaps the attachment between them had faded and this was a chance to revisit a childish fancy?

Oh, she was grasping at straws! Let her be honest. It would suit her all too well if Lady Selina was truly in love with another. Not that Justin could be hers if the creature did cry off. But the tiny vestige of hope was enough for her to weave a fantasy to fit her dreams.

It would not do to dwell on it. Nor should she interfere. To speak of it would put the cat among the pigeons, and for what? Even had she gauged the situation with accuracy, it was better for Justin to remain in ignorance. She might trust Lady Selina to behave with circumspection, for she had been hasty enough to gloss over the incident.

Thus decided, Marianne brought her attention to bear on choosing a novel for Grace, and thrust the matter to the back of her mind. Where it remained, niggling and malignant, like a spider watching for its prey.

# Chapter Seven

Although Marianne necessarily met with Lady Selina once or twice at events where she chaperoned Jocasta, she saw no sign of the mysterious colonel. As Lady Selina was invariably accompanied by Justin this was scarcely surprising. But at a soirée given by Mrs Guineaford, which Grace refused to attend on the score that the woman had stayed away from her own musical evening, she noticed Gregory O'Donovan among the coterie of gentlemen surrounding the beauty.

Her attention caught, she watched for any sign of tenderness or contact between them. It was many days since she had caught them in Hookham's together, in an obviously clandestine meeting. Yet here he was, openly forming one of her court.

Her gaze intent, Marianne noted how his eyes strayed to Lady Selina each time she laughed, although he was engaged in conversation with one of the other gentlemen around her. Elegant as ever in a silver spotted robe over a muslin gown, Selina appeared to be in spirits, exchanging banter impartially with one or other of her cavaliers. But not once with the colonel. Did that bode ill or well?

Marianne returned her attention to him. Was he a trifle stiff? Unlike the fellow he was talking to, he did not look relaxed. Or was it merely a military bearing?

She was just wondering where Justin was in all this when he spoke immediately behind her.

"Taken a fancy to a redcoat, have you, Marianne?"

She jumped, turning to face him. He was grinning down at her with that teasing glint in his eye she knew so well. Her heartbeat became instantly irregular and her breath caught in her chest.

"Nothing of the sort," she managed, her mind half frozen. Heavens, what could she say? How to explain why she was staring so hard?

Justin did not appear to notice her condition. "A dashing fellow, isn't he? I'd have thought it might appeal to you to follow the drum, with your family history."

"Papa was in the Navy, and before you ask, I don't hanker for a life at sea either." She spoke with more instinct than ease, but he laughed. Her relief was short-lived.

"Shall I tell Selina to relinquish him to you? She can afford to lose at least one of her cicisbeos."

Marianne could not prevent the words from leaving her lips. "Don't you mind?"

His brows rose. "Should I? Isn't it the height of fashion to have one's betrothed sought after by other men?"

"Is it? I hadn't noticed."

The smile left his eyes and his lip curled. "Don't be naïve, Marianne. You are aware of the circumstances."

Her heart ached for him. More so with the secret suspicion she cherished. "Meaning you don't care."

"Meaning I care very much indeed, but we are none of us masters of our fate."

The bitter note was unmistakable. She toyed briefly with the notion of speaking up. If it would procure his release, did she not owe him that loyalty? If only she could be sure she had not imagined it.

"You are very thoughtful. What is it, Marianne?"

The gentler note cut her to shreds. What in the world was she to say? She improvised. "Oh, I … I was thinking of Jocasta. She has shown no preference, but I'm afraid Cousin

Grace has decided views on who will suit. I only hope the poor girl is not thrust into marriage with … with…"

"With a man she cannot care for?" His voice was hard. "Have no fear. Any suitor must pass through me before she can marry. I won't let her be made unhappy, be sure."

"Yes, I had forgot you are her guardian. Of course you won't."

Her response was mechanical. His own obvious unhappiness raked her, raising again the dread question dividing her mind. Should she warn him? Or would that be to bring a world of trouble tumbling down upon his head?

She was no nearer a decision a few mornings later when Lady Sessay came to call upon Grace with the object of discussing wedding plans. Gowned in an overdress of pink and black striped satin, she put Grace's plain blue gown into the shade. But her manner was perfectly amiable and not at all patronising.

"For I could not proceed, my dear Lady Purford, without consulting your convenience."

Not much to Marianne's surprise, Grace became flustered.

"Oh! How kind, only I don't know — Justin has not said anything to me."

Lady Sessay smiled but Marianne saw no pleasure in her at mention of her prospective son-in-law.

"Lord Purford is content to leave the matter in our hands, he told me. Gentlemen, in any event, are not much in the way of participating in these arrangements."

"But it is his wedding," Grace protested.

Marianne judged it to be time for a rescue. She forced a laugh. "Now, ma'am, you know Justin is no hand at such arrangements. One has simply to set all in train and remind him to appear on the day."

Grace looked relieved and troubled all at the same time. "That is true indeed. He can never be got to involve himself in domestic issues."

Like his stepmother, Marianne could have said. It was plain she must take a hand. "Have you decided upon a particular day, Lady Sessay?"

"I have several in mind, but I would not settle the date before discovering if it will suit Lady Purford."

Grace looked rather helplessly at Marianne. Nothing was further from Marianne's desire than to become involved in the preparations for Justin's nuptials to another woman, but duty beckoned.

In the event, once the date was settled, she and Grace had nothing to do but agree to the various queries Lady Sessay put forward since she had clearly determined the entire proceedings before coming to Purford House. Guessing she would be put out by a request to change any of the details, Marianne offered none. Truth to tell, she was in too great a state of shock to think properly.

The only change she truly wished for was a complete cancellation. Her heart shied at the early date selected. June! A rapid calculation told her it was less than six weeks away. Such haste was almost unseemly. Was Lady Sessay so intent on securing Justin that she did not dare give him time to retract?

It was also extremely inconvenient. How in the world were they to prepare Purford Park for the reception of its new mistress in such a short space of time?

This question occupied her through most of Lady Sessay's visit, and she took it up as soon as that lady departed.

"You know, ma'am, we ought to have objected to the date."

Grace's face fell. "Oh, Marianne, no! I supposed you must know we had no engagement on that day."

"We don't, but it's much too soon, cousin. Unless Justin and Lady Selina are intent upon a prolonged honeymoon."

"Good heavens, do you think so? I should not have supposed either would be wishing to be alone together for long. I mean, they scarcely live in each other's pockets. They might have been married for years!"

This observation did nothing for Marianne's peace of mind, sending her thoughts flying back to the matter of the scarlet-coated cavalier. She forced them back. The wedding was in train and there was nothing to be done about it now.

"We will ask Justin. The wedding may be the business of the Sessays, but he can't ignore what happens afterwards."

"You may ask him, Marianne, for I cannot. Only conceive how embarrassing!"

Marianne gave an inward sigh. She would not only be obliged to put the question herself, she would likely have to suggest where he should take the creature. As if she cared! But that was scarcely the point.

"However much time they may spend away, cousin, the fact remains they will return to Purford Park and no preparations have been made for Lady Selina's reception."

Grace's face of dismay was almost ludicrous. "Oh, dear. Oh, Marianne, what are we to do?"

"It is rather more a matter of what needs to be done. At the very least, we must make her apartments ready."

"Oh, dear. Thank goodness I moved out of them after dear Edmund passed on."

"You could scarcely have remained after Justin took up residence, since they adjoin his. But that bedchamber has not been used for years and it is bound to be musty."

Grace began to look as harried as Marianne felt. "And Mrs Woofferton is here with us. Oh, Marianne, whatever shall we do?"

There was no question what must be done. Within three days, Marianne departed for Purford Park, accompanied by the housekeeper, on a mission to make all ready for the new mistress of the house, a task she regarded with a mixture of loathing and despair.

By dint of putting pressure on a number of persons, Marianne succeeded in transforming not only the bedchamber which was to house the new Countess of Purford, but the dressing-room and parlour as well. With no notion of what Lady Selina might like, she had thought only of a suitable setting for her elegance and beauty.

With insufficient time to apply to the fashionable London suppliers, she was obliged to rely upon the estate carpenters, the village sewing women and the linen-draper in Woking. The four-poster had been polished, stripped of its old hangings and the ugly tester replaced. All the rugs were taken out and beaten, the floors scrubbed, the cracks in the walls re-plastered and painted over, the window blinds dusted.

Marianne ransacked the unoccupied bedchambers, and was able to exchange the plain old press for one with an ornamental inlay. Discarded in the attics, she found a pretty long mirror with very little spotting which she caused to be transported to the dressing-room, along with a landscape painting to be set above the chaise longue on the parlour wall.

While Marianne planned and directed, Mrs Woofferton bustled, setting all available hands to clean and polish in all three rooms. By the third week, Marianne was able to breathe again, feeling everything was being done that could be done to effect what was necessarily a makeshift change. No doubt Lady Selina would have her own ideas, but at least Grace would have nothing to blush for and Justin might bring his bride home to a welcoming environment.

She was just finishing a luncheon of simple fare — for the servants were so busy she had insisted upon informality for the moment — when Mrs Woofferton came in to tell her the sewing women had finished.

"The men are hanging the curtains, Miss Marianne, and I thought you'd like to see how they look."

"I would indeed, Mrs Woofferton. I will come directly."

She was eager to see the effect, for she had selected a very pretty pattern for the new bed hangings, which was a little out of the way. It was one of the most expensive in Mr Petherick's shop, but Marianne had been drawn to it despite feeling it might be a little too frivolous for Lady Selina. She had pored over a number of more traditional brocades and velvets, but her eye kept returning to this particular one and in the end she had allowed her partiality to rule.

By the time she got to the chamber, the hangings were up and drawn around the bed. Marianne stopped on the threshold, feeling an unexpected pang as a memory leapt in her mind.

The bright pattern of birds intertwined with leaves and vines was almost identical to that on the bed-curtains she'd had as a child when her parents were alive.

Guilt and dismay swamped her. How had she been so imprudent? All unknowing, she had imposed her own nostalgia upon Lady Selina. As if this was her bed, her chamber, her place in Justin's life!

"Do you not like it after all, Miss Marianne?"

The disappointment in Mrs Woofferton's voice cut into her shock. Marianne pulled herself together.

"Yes, indeed I do." Far too much, if she spoke truth. "It was just … I had not expected it to make up so well."

The three sewing women from the village were looking anxious, clearly awaiting her verdict. Marianne smiled and went forward to clasp each of their hands in turn.

"Thank you so much. You have made a wonderful job of it. And so quickly too! I cannot thank you enough. Be sure your diligence and support will be reflected in the fees for your services."

Beaming with pleasure, the women thanked her for having been given the opportunity. Thrusting her dismay out of mind, Marianne took time to examine the hangings closely so that she might admire their stitchery. She was perfectly aware, as were they, that such a task would not have come their way in the normal course of events, and the extra income would be only too welcome.

The curtains were then drawn back and tied so Marianne could see the effect for the daylight hours. She expressed herself as being delighted with the result, even as the sight of the new quilt she had bought told her she'd been guilty of yet more nostalgia. It was precisely the warm gold colour she'd had in the little house where she and Mama (alone for the most part with Papa away at sea) had lived in Portsmouth, and blended perfectly with the pale gold ground of the hangings.

The sewing women curtsied themselves out under Mrs Woofferton's escort. The men had already left and Marianne was alone in the chamber at last.

She could not resist touching the fabric of the hangings, running her fingers over the flying birds as she had done when it lay on Mr Petherick's counter along with the other options she had considered. Memories flooded her mind.

Sitting up in her bed, drinking the hot sweet tea Mama permitted her the time she was ill with influenza. A rare luxury, for Mama kept the precious tea for visitors as a rule… Giggling and shrieking as she wriggled all over the quilt when Papa tickled her without mercy, in a bid to leave her with a happy memory as he always did each time his ship was due to depart… Clinging to the bed-post, sobbing into the curtains on the dreadful day she knew he would never come home again…

Marianne's throat tightened and she released her hold on the curtains. This would not do. She had not thought of the old days for years and this was no moment to be raking them up.

Nevertheless she could not withstand a surge of resentment that Lady Selina would inhabit this bower with all its unconscious contact with her own past. She had only herself to blame. So stupid not to realise, to allow herself an impossible indulgence.

Well, it was too late now to change it. She must console herself with the reflection that none but she need ever know. Nor was it likely she would enter the chamber once Lady Selina was installed in her personal apartments.

"Miss Marianne?"

Guiltily snatching her hand away from the fabric, she turned to face Sprake. The under butler had charge of the household in Rowsham's absence, and had been a rock in this crisis. She smiled.

"Will you tell the men how grateful I am for all their help, Sprake? They have done so well, don't you think?"

The man bowed. "Very well, miss."

She then noticed the silver salver which bore a folded paper, and took in that Sprake was looking a trifle grave. "What is it?"

"An express from London, Miss Marianne. It was delivered but a moment ago. I thought it right to bring it straight to you."

A flitter of unease ran through Marianne as she went towards him. What now? What was so urgent that one of the family must send to her now? "Is it from his lordship?"

"It is franked by Lord Luthrie, miss."

Marianne stared even as she reached out for the sealed letter. "Lord Luthrie?"

Then it must be from Justin's aunt. Unprecedented. What in the world had happened? "Thank you, Sprake."

She broke the seal as the butler bowed and departed, her mind leaping with possibilities. Her pulse began to thrum as the horrid image of Justin either dead or injured flitted through her mind. Or was it Grace? She could think of no other reason for Lady Luthrie to be writing to her.

She unfolded the single sheet, only half aware of moving back towards the familiarity and comfort of the bed with its fatal new hangings.

"*My dear Marianne…*" Her eye swept to the end. "*In haste … Philippa Luthrie.*"

The paper quivered as Marianne's fingers began to shake. Her eyes flew back to the start and she ran them rapidly down the sheet, hardly able to take in the words.

Not Justin, no. Lady Selina? No! She was gone … *dreadful scandal … an obscure colonel…* Oh, dear Lord, it must be the fellow she'd met in Hookham's! She should have warned Justin…

The horrid word jumped at her from the page. *Eloped!* Lady Selina had eloped with Gregory O'Donovan.

"*…branding herself a jilt and exposing Justin to the mockery of the ton.*"

Marianne's legs weakened. She sought the bed and sat down, her spotted muslin skirts spreading about her, and stared at the words that appeared to run into one another on the page. Her vision blurred.

No! She must not faint!

She looked up, away from the paper, deliberately seeking some other view to re-orient herself. She breathed deeply, trying for a measure of calm.

But it was difficult to remain calm when her treacherous blood was soaring with joy. Aware it was deeply inappropriate, Marianne fought to control the feeling. There was nothing joyful in this hideous news.

Her eye fell again to the letter.

"*Grace is prostrate, as you may imagine, and determined to run away. Which is why I have written to you, Marianne. Your calm good sense is needed.*"

Calm good sense? Good heavens! She was anything but calm and her good sense had wholly deserted her. All she could think about was the desperate hope encompassed in the fact that Justin was free.

"*It is vital the family remains in Town to face down the gossips. For Jocasta's sake, if nothing else. The child is doing very well, holding her head up, even though she realises the harm this may do her.*"

But what of Justin? How has he taken it? Marianne saw his name, but looked in vain for any mention of his emotions.

"*I must beg you to return with all speed, Marianne. Do not delay when Justin comes to fetch you. I can make no headway with Grace but I know she will listen to you.*"

Anger began to seep into Marianne's already conflicted emotions. Did Justin not matter in all this? He was the one most hurt by it. He must be determined to face it out. Why could not Lady Luthrie make him the subject of her panic?

The letter dropped to her lap, clutched in tense fingers. Was he distressed? Elated? Relieved?

No, how could he be anything but hurt and angry? Exposed to the mockery of the ton, his aunt said. Oh, he must be smarting in his pride indeed! To have waited so long, allowing the gossips to speculate, and then to have thrown the handkerchief only to be made to look a fool when the lady of his choice rejected him for another. And in such a way. Mortifying indeed! To fly from her home, her standing in Society, to her own ruin? How desperately must Lady Selina love her colonel to have courage enough to flout convention.

From pity and anger on Justin's behalf, Marianne veered suddenly to admiration for Lady Selina. Did it not take courage to abandon all she knew and set herself outside her social circle, all for the sake of love? She had fought for her future, for her happiness.

Marianne could not aspire to such valour. Had she made the slightest push to secure her own happiness? No, she had not. Deciding her case was hopeless, she had put all her efforts into concealment, determined to endure. Lady Selina's action made her feel a ninny. She could not approve it, for it had hurt Justin and put Jocasta's chances in jeopardy. But as a woman, she could not but applaud so fierce a resolve to secure what clearly mattered too deeply to be set aside.

She became aware of her surroundings, her eye falling upon the freshly white-washed walls, the polished wood surrounds to the sparkling windows and the beautifully renewed bed upon which she was sitting.

A flood of dismay attacked her. All this work, all this effort and expense, and all to go to waste. Who knew when Justin might marry now? It was doubtful he would soon seek another prospective countess after this disaster. Unless...

The snaking notion crept through the barriers she had herself set up and sprang full-blown into her head, shocking her with its intensity.

No, she could not! Impossible. Yet if she failed to seize this opportunity, it might never come again. Her heart knocked sickeningly in her bosom. He was coming to fetch her, Lady Luthrie said. What better chance?

Seize the day? She could not do it. She was not like Lady Selina. She could never find the courage.

Or could she?

# Chapter Eight

The weather being a trifle warmer, Justin had elected to drive himself. If, at the back of his mind, he'd hoped having something to do would prevent his thoughts from straying, he was disappointed. Despite the necessity to guide his team through the press of traffic in the post towns, there was all too much leisure as he drove through the quieter country roads.

His memory dwelled obstinately on the events of the day Lord Sessay had summoned him to the house in Grosvenor Square.

He'd entered the morning room to find his prospective father-in-law looking worn and grave, while Lady Sessay, thoroughly out of character, sat huddled on a sofa, weeping into a handkerchief.

Shocked conjecture rode Justin. What in the world had occurred to cast the couple into such affliction? He did not wait for his host to begin. "What is amiss, sir?" The absence of his betrothed threw him into instant concern. "Is it Selina? Has some accident befallen?"

"Not an accident, no." Lord Sessay brought forth a heavy sigh. "But it is indeed Selina."

A wail from the sofa alarmed Justin.

"What, is she injured? Dead? Pray don't spare me, sir, but tell me at once!"

"She is alive and well, as far as I can say. Yet I hardly know how to tell you. Won't you sit down, my boy?"

"Thank you, sir, but if you are big with dismaying news as I suspect, I would prefer to stand."

Lord Sessay crossed to a side table where a supply of decanters stood on a tray. "Let me offer you a restorative, for you will need it."

"I need nothing, sir, for the moment. Pray enlighten me, for the suspense is more than I can bear."

Another heavy sigh and Lord Sessay came across to lay a hand on Justin's shoulder.

"Never did I think to be obliged to confess such a dreadful thing to you, Purford. I cannot sufficiently regret it, and I blame myself. I ought to have warned you the moment the fellow appeared in Town."

Justin's heartbeat accelerated. "Fellow?"

"There is no point in concealment. A prior attachment. We had supposed it long over. Selina gave no indication — she was determined to be dutiful —"

Hope began to filter into Justin's lacerated emotions. "Are you saying she wishes to cry off?"

Lady Sessay's sobs redoubled and her lord fetched another deep sigh.

"It is a great deal worse than that, my boy. My wretched daughter has eloped with the fellow."

Justin recalled little of what followed in the immediate aftermath of hearing the fell tidings. A glass of wine had been thrust upon him and he'd tossed it off, listening with half an ear to his host's apologetic harangue, his lady's intermittent sobs a vague irritant in the background.

His first reaction had been one of staggering relief. Until the thought of the public consequences began to seep through. He had swung from relief to fury to apprehension, back and forth, as a mechanical part of his mind made appropriate enquiries.

Had any effort been made to recover Selina? None, Lord Sessay told him, for what was the point when the escape had been effected early the day before? Selina had duped her parents finely, pretending she was going on a visit to her former governess at a slight distance from London, which would necessitate staying the night. Her maid had accompanied her, and been sent back alone in the coach that morning, armed with the fatal letter.

Selina and Colonel O'Donovan had driven to Dover the previous day and boarded a packet, leaving the maid and coachman innocently waiting at an inn near the governess's cottage. On returning to fetch her mistress, the maid found her gone, the governess ignorant of everything except the letter she had been charged to keep until a girl came for it upon the following day. By the time the news reached Sessay House, the errant couple, if they had carried out the intentions outlined in Selina's letter, were already in France and very likely married.

Lord Sessay's distress had aged him in a bang, Justin thought, recalling the man's grey and crumpled features. His apologetic anxiety grated.

"What do you wish, my boy? You are shocked, angry, and with good reason. We are in your hands. The story cannot but leak out, there is no holding such a piece of news."

At that, a fresh wail emanated from her ladyship. "Oh, the scandal! She has ruined herself — and us too!"

"Yes, yes, my dear Caroline, but we are here concerned with Purford, you know."

Sessay went to pat his helpmeet in an ineffective way, casting an imploring look upon Justin, who shrugged away the chaotic confusion of his thoughts.

"My dear sir, pray don't trouble yourself on my account. I can stand a knock or two." He drew a breath. "To be truthful with you, it struck me more than once that Selina was not completely happy in our engagement."

Lord Sessay waved distracted hands. "However that may be, it cannot excuse her conduct now. I am deeply disappointed."

Justin did not say what he suspected. That the Sessays had brought pressure to bear upon Selina to accept his suit. Nor could he disclose his own true feelings upon the event. He compromised. "I understand you, sir, and I could wish Selina had confided in me. I would not have held her to her promise had I known her heart was given to another."

His lordship came across and seized his hand, squeezing it hard. "Your sentiments do you credit, Purford, uncommonly good of you."

The fellow's eyes were suspiciously bright, and Justin made haste to turn the subject. "Perhaps we had best turn our attention to how we may evade the interest of the vulgar."

Sessay released him, sighing again. "I fear there is no such recourse, my boy. My wife is too distressed to be troubled with whispers and question. I shall take her home to Yorkshire."

Was that wise? To flee the aftermath?

"Will that not make things worse, sir? I propose to put a notice in the papers to the effect that the betrothal is at an end."

At that, Lady Sessay spoke up, her voice shrill, redolent with despair. "Of what use to say so, when everyone will know the worst?"

"Hush, my love, don't upset yourself. Purford is doing his best, you know."

Justin addressed himself to both impartially, a seed of hope entering his mind. "We will not silence gossiping tongues, ma'am, but what if you were to insert a notice to the effect that Lady Selina was married privately to Colonel O'Donovan and has departed for the continent upon a prolonged honeymoon?"

Lady Sessay's blotched countenance abruptly lost its woebegone air, and her lord looked as if he had been struck in the back of the head.

Justin pursued his advantage. "If we pretend the affair has been arranged and sanctioned by all parties, Selina may return one day and re-establish her position in Society. You cannot wish, I am persuaded, to be forever estranged from your daughter."

His words were having an effect, both parents evidently turning them over. Lord Sessay was the first to recover his astonishment, and was moved to shake Justin by the hand again. "By George, you have a head on your shoulders, my boy! And a generous spirit. Few men would be as forgiving."

Justin disclaimed, disturbed by a sliver of guilt. Easy to forgive when the desperate act had effected his release.

"As if anyone will believe it!"

These bitter words caused Sessay to return to the sofa. "It does not signify, Caroline. For my part, I believe Purford's scheme may save us all."

Lady Sessay uttered a moan. "All is in train for the wedding too!"

It occurred to Justin that Colonel O'Donovan's appearance in Town had been responsible for the early date of the wedding proposed by Lady Sessay. Had she even then been afraid Selina's partiality might cause her to cry off? If only she had!

"Well, we must cancel the arrangements," Lord Sessay was saying. "We will naturally cover the expenses incurred for such work as has been already done, but that is a trifling cost compared to the disaster we will face but for Purford's grace-saving notion."

"Will you remain in Town then, sir?"

His lordship's reply was forestalled by his wife's objection.

"And face everyone as if nothing has occurred?"

"No, indeed, ma'am, that would be impossible. But a united front will do better for us, I believe, than a concerted departure."

Lady Sessay looked unconvinced, and indeed it was doubtful she would be fit to be seen for several days. Her lord undertook to send the necessary notice and, having settled matters as best he could under the circumstances, Justin was at last able to take his leave.

His thoughts immediately fell back into chaos until he remembered that he must give his family the news.

The effect was, if anything, worse than it had been upon himself. He found Grace in the morning room, having just received two callers. Justin sent for his sister and ordered Rowsham to deny her ladyship to any more visitors.

Jocasta had been stunned into silence for several moments, staring at him as if she could not believe her ears. Grace, on the other hand, had all but swooned and had to be helped to the sofa, where she lay in a semi-prostrate condition, sniffing at the vinaigrette which was never far from her reach.

The scheme of relief Justin propounded was met with horror.

"I cannot, Justin," declared Grace, emerging briefly from the vinaigrette. "Face all the sly looks and comments of the curious? The dreadful faces of disapproval of those censorious creatures who will delight at my downfall?" She shuddered.

"If it is what Justin wishes, Mama, then you must."

Jocasta came to him, catching at one of his hands and holding it tight, her eyes swimming as she met his gaze. "Justin, I'm so sorry. It's horrid for you. How dared Selina serve you such a trick? Why could she not have spoken before?"

Justin winced. "I wish she had done so, but I suspect she was coerced."

His sister's eyes widened as the wet receded. "What, you mean she was forced into accepting your offer?"

"Worse. I think her parents had forbidden her to think of O'Donovan at the outset."

"Because she was meant for you?"

"I dare say that was part of it."

Jocasta released his hand, disgust entering her lively features. "How gothic!"

He was obliged to smile. "Rather mercenary than gothic, I fear."

"You mean ambitious! This colonel was not considered good enough for Selina, I suppose. If he had been titled and rich, your claim would have been set aside."

Her indignation lightened his mood. He could not but be amused.

"I'm not sure I had a claim, Jocasta."

"Well, you considered it a strong enough reason not to wish to marry anyone else."

"What does it signify?" demanded Grace from the sofa. "Nothing signifies in the face of the appalling scandal — and we will all partake of it. Your suitors will shab off as fast as they can, for no man will care to be associated with —"

"Grace, that's enough!"

Angry now, Justin caught Jocasta by the shoulders as her face fell in ludicrous dismay. "Don't be alarmed, my lovely. That is precisely why we must adhere to my plan and remain in the public eye. We will brave it through in the teeth of them all and you will see how quickly it will be forgotten."

"Forgotten? It will never be forgotten! Our family name will be forever tainted."

Grace burst into tears after this declaration, and Justin was obliged to bite back the blistering reproof hovering on his tongue.

He found Jocasta eyeing him in a troubled way.

"Will it taint us? Can we hope to rise above it?"

"We must. For your sake as well as my own. Have you any engagement this evening?"

A tearful interruption came from Grace before Jocasta could reply. "Pray don't expect me to make an appearance in public this evening! I could not do it. Oh, if only Marianne were here!"

Marianne! In all the distortion of his immediate life, Justin had forgotten her absence — slaving away at Purford Park to make the place habitable for Selina. Hell's teeth! Was there no end to the repercussions?

He decided then and there to go home and fetch Marianne back to Town. It was evident Grace would need her support.

One more necessary visit had to be made, however, before anything else could be done. Pausing only to write the notice to be inserted into the principal London journals and send it off with Simon the footman, he walked round to the Luthrie's town house in Berkeley Square.

His aunt, while shocked and incredulous, proved sturdier than his stepmother. When he told her how cast down Grace was, she immediately offered to add her weight to his arguments.

"I will try what I can do, Justin. You have taken a sensible route and I believe it will answer. But it is imperative we stand together."

"Just so, ma'am. If you can prevail upon Grace to drop her megrims and appear in public, I will be eternally grateful."

"Well, I will do my best. But to say truth, there is only one person who is likely to make headway with Grace."

He smiled. "I know it, ma'am. I will have to show my face around town for a day or two, but I aim to fetch Marianne as soon as I can decently leave without the gossips accusing me of running away."

He had taken care to do the rounds of his clubs, ensuring that when the news broke it would be known he had been acting with perfect normality that day. His cousin Alexander, who had been sitting with his mother at the time and was necessarily in the secret, accompanied him to Brooks's. Lord Dymond, heir to his father's ancient earldom as well as the baronetage of Luthrie, bore an invented courtesy title made up of the family name. He was a pleasant and popular companion, a couple of years Justin's junior, but very much his friend as well as a fond cousin and Justin was glad of his support.

In the evening, although Grace could not be prevailed upon to leave the house, Justin commandeered the services of the Dragon and escorted his sister to a party where it was evident the news had broken. The looks from behind fans were both curious and pitying. One or two gentlemen stared openly; others made a pretence of ignorance, but could not wholly disguise their consciousness.

Jocasta bore up well, holding her head high and behaving with a courageous semblance of her usual vivacity. By good fortune, their cousin Lord Dymond was at the same party and he solicited her for a dance. This broke the ice and she received several more invitations.

Justin breathed more easily, although he had to endure a number of enquiries about Grace's whereabouts. He countered with a spurious tale of an indisposition, and nearly lost his temper when Mrs Guineaford greeted his explanation with a contemptuous and disbelieving lift of the eyebrows.

Upon the following evening, he met with the Sessays at a musical evening, their notice having appeared along with his own in the London journals. Lady Sessay was proudly erect, although there was a tell-tale quiver in her fingers as she clasped Justin's.

"Very well done, Justin, my boy," murmured her lord. "It is hard, but we will contrive to brush through."

He agreed to it, and was glad when the entertainment began and he need not keep up the act. That it was taking a toll on his emotions he did not realise until he was actually in his phaeton on the way to Purford Park.

Relieved of the necessity to keep his countenance, he was assailed by visions of the faces he had encountered over the past few days. They had not silenced the gossips by any means, though none dared say anything directly to those concerned. Lady Luthrie, deep in her friend Lady Sessay's confidence, reported that she and her lord had received no congratulations on Selina's marriage, which proved conclusively that no one yet understood the story they had concocted.

Justin had set his cousin and aunt to put the tale about, in the hopes it would spread. However, since Grace was still refusing to appear in public and had declared her unalterable intention to return home, he could no longer delay his proposed trip to bring Marianne back to London.

The journey occupied too many hours for his comfort, since he found himself at last giving way to the conflicting emotions of the last hideous days.

It struck him that in all the turmoil of his thoughts, never once did they turn to Selina. A creeping realisation made him recognise how narrow an escape he'd had. He had been about to commit his entire life to a woman he could neither love nor admire. She was beautiful enough, but her character and his were so opposed they must have ended in complete indifference.

Had he even known her? Her prickly attitude was now explained, but he found it hard to forgive her for not telling him the truth when he gave her the chance. He would have been spared the indignity he must suffer in the face of her scandalous flight. He'd done what he could to scotch it, but in his heart of hearts he knew he must still be an object of compassion, which stuck in his throat. If he'd wanted to marry Selina, he could have borne it better. But to be thought to be distraught when in fact he was rather elated, was galling in the extreme.

His pride had suffered a blow from which it would be hard to recover. Only now, when he had no need to conceal his feelings under an iron front, did the smart begin in earnest.

# Chapter Nine

"You look dreadful."

The drawn look in Justin's face lightened briefly, his eyes crinkling at the corners.

"I knew I might depend on your tact, Marianne."

She laughed, curling away the distress in a corner of her bosom, along with the nervous apprehension with which she'd awaited his coming. "Go and get rid of the travel stains and I'll engage to cosset you with food, wine and as much sympathy as you can take."

"That sounds deliciously comforting."

Marianne found her fingers in his, and they tingled as he dropped a light kiss on them.

She watched him ascend the stairs, her heart catching as she saw how heavily he trod. Then she slipped into the cosy breakfast parlour where, at her request, the under-butler was directing the maids in the preparation of luncheon.

"His lordship has gone up to refresh himself, Sprake. I don't imagine he will be much above a half hour."

She then repaired to the morning room across the hall, there to try and steady her jumping nerves. She must ascertain Justin's state of mind before she could think of having a touch at her own fate. Yet if the moment should seem propitious —

Her mind balked. The first sight of him had sent a jolt of dismay through her. She had not supposed him to have been in love with Lady Selina, but his aspect was awful. If his heart was truly broken, she could not hope to carry out the ill-formed notion that refused to lie down and be quiet. Ever since it had

73

entered her head, she had been by turns in alt at the possibility and sheer terror at the thought of what she must do.

She drew a calming breath and resolved to do nothing. She was not now concerned with herself, but with Justin. That he needed her was evident. She would not deny him the solace of her friendship.

He did not keep her waiting long, and while they ate in the presence of the servants, talk was necessarily confined to commonplaces. As a result, Marianne noted his stiffness and the effort he was making to appear normal.

By the time they rose from the table, she had made up her mind. "Sprake, will you tell his lordship's valet to bring down his coat, if you please. And have someone fetch me a cloak as well."

Justin frowned as the under-butler went off on his errand. "What's to do?"

"We're going for a walk."

"Are we?"

"It's windy enough to blow your crotchets away."

He let out a sound, half snort, half laughter. "That might take a hurricane."

"Well, I dare say I can arrange for one, if it should prove necessary."

He did laugh at that. "Nothing defeats you, Marianne, does it?"

All too much defeated her, but she did not say so.

For some few minutes, they walked without speaking, heading by common consent for the old oak at the edge of the woods which had ever been their point of rendezvous.

Justin broke the silence. "How much do you know?"

"The bare facts, I imagine. I had an express from Lady Luthrie the day before yesterday."

He glanced at her, and Marianne saw the frown.

"She told you I was coming to get you?"

"And begged me to return with all speed."

He looked away. "I hope you will consent, Marianne, or Grace may undo us all."

"I will do whatever is needed."

He paused in his way and turned to look at her. Marianne found contrition in his eyes and her breath tightened.

"You never disappoint, Marianne. We have used you shamefully, all of us."

She became at once brusque, unable to bear his distress. "Fiddle! None of you ever treated me as less than one of the family, and I've done my part, that's all."

He sought and found her hands, holding them hard, the green eyes reflecting more emotion than she had ever seen in him.

"It is not all. Devil take it, Aunt Pippa was right! Your future should have been looked to, and instead, here you are slaving to make those wretched apartments habitable, and all for nothing."

She winced. "Yes, I confess that rather leapt to my eye as well, but it is a small matter after all." She saw his mouth open to argue and returned the pressure of his fingers briefly. "Don't, Justin. I am far less concerned with wasted effort than with your situation."

With a sigh, he released her. "To tell you the truth, Marianne, I no longer know how to think about my situation."

"I don't wonder at it," she returned, beginning to walk again and urging him onward with a touch at his sleeve. "What precisely happened?"

With mixed feelings, she listened to a stilted account of the past few days. Guilt reared its head again when she heard how neatly Lady Selina had planned her escape. Had there been further clandestine meetings after that one in Hookham's? She had seen how the couple conducted themselves in public. Such detailed arrangements could not have been settled except in a series of tête-à-têtes.

Should she confess to Justin? Yet what good would it do? More likely it would do harm, adding to his burden of conflicted emotions. That he was, as expected, both hurt and angry was evident in the manner of his recital, but Marianne could not judge whether his heart was touched.

By the time she was acquainted with all the details of his activities before he left London, they were seated upon the bench that had been cunningly built to incorporate the trunk of the ancient oak. With her cloak to protect her old round gown of brown muslin, she was unconcerned with possible stains, and besides too intent to care.

Justin fell silent and Marianne watched him for a moment, her heart wrung at his aspect. He sat a couple of feet away, his great-coat hanging open as he leaned his arms on his thighs, staring at the ground between his booted feet.

She had never seen him look so dejected and it drove from her mind any thought but that of easing him. The words were out before she could think about the wisdom of uttering them.

"Do you love her, Justin?"

He reared up, turning to stare at her with knit brows and an expression hard to read.

"Selina? Good Lord, no!"

Her heart jerked uncontrollably and then settled to a thrum that pounded in her breast. She could not speak.

Justin looked away, his gaze roving lawns dotted with batches of trees and interrupted by the swirl of the lake. From here the house sprawled across the horizon, with its round bays situated where the later wings began either side of the long portico with the covered walkway, the central high original part of the building dominating above. Sheep grazed near the trees, and a stray deer from the Crail herds wandered across the grass.

How much of his domain did Justin see? He looked to have his thoughts turned inwards. Marianne was startled when he spoke, a harsh note in his voice.

"What rankles is the hypocrisy, the deliberate deceit. When I think how I waited to be sure Selina's fancy did not light upon another — and for what? Even when we became betrothed and her manner towards me showed her indifference — worse indeed, for I thought often she actually disliked me — she kept silent."

Beside him, Marianne remained still, unwilling to interrupt the flow, damping down a rising snake of fury.

"I taxed her with having formed another attachment, but she denied it. And the Sessays knew! When he summoned me, Lord Sessay was so put about, he mentioned the matter."

"He told you?"

"He said he thought the affair had been long forgotten, but I don't believe that. In light of events, it's obvious to me Selina's parents forbade her to think of this fellow, just as my father — "

He broke off and Marianne's heart did a little flip, a hideous conjecture leaping in her mind. Had Justin nourished a secret passion too?

"What I mean is," he resumed, a trifle stiff, "I think Selina was subject to this intolerable scheme concocted by our sires. Coerced by it, in fact. She made no secret of her reluctance to wed me. She charged me to cease any pretence that either of us would have chosen the other, had we followed our inclination."

"Was that true?" It was out before Marianne could stop it.

He gave a harsh laugh. "Evidently."

"Of you, I mean."

He turned to look at her then, a glare in his eyes. Marianne could not tell if it was directed at the ghost of Lady Selina or herself.

"Don't be a ninny! Of course it was. When I said I waited, I really meant I was hoping Selina would choose another man."

"Yet you courted her last year, or so it was reported to Grace."

Justin threw back his head in a well-remembered gesture of defiance. "My father left me no choice. I knew the Sessays expected me to honour the arrangement. I thought if I got to know the girl, spent time with her, we might discover ourselves to be mutually agreeable."

"You didn't expect to fall in love with her then?"

The glare returned to her face. "I wish you will not keep harping on it, Marianne. Do you suppose I was brought up to pay any mind to such rubbishing romantical notions? I'm an earl, for pity's sake! I am obliged to marry a female with appropriate status and background."

Marianne's secret hope took a dive, but she rallied. "In this day and age? We do not live in the Dark Ages, Justin. I have heard of several instances of peers marrying to please themselves."

"And thereby bringing their title and name into disrepute," he said, the bitter note pronounced.

"That doesn't appear to be confined to marrying beneath them."

The instant the words were out of her mouth, she regretted them. Too late.

"I thank you, Marianne. Just the reminder I needed."

She winced. "Well, I'm sorry, but I do think you are being ridiculous. I dare say there are a score of eligible ladies you might marry, if you chose."

"I dare say there are, but —"

"And since the earl's daughter picked out for you is no longer available, you ought to be thanking your stars that you can now choose."

"Don't you think I have been? Dear Lord, I was so relieved when I heard the news, I wanted to shout it to the world!"

"Except that the world is apt to shout back."

He let out one of his snorting laughs. "You are nothing if not candid, Marianne. I thought you brought me out here to sympathise."

She had to smile. "So I did. But you will scarcely expect me to keep quiet when you talk such nonsense."

He grinned. "No, you never could keep your mouth shut, horrible girl! I don't know why I bear with you."

Marianne warmed inside. Unwittingly, she had provoked him into dropping the reserve he'd worn with her for so long.

"Someone has to keep you in line," she said, in the bantering tone to which he'd ever responded.

"Any more, and you'll be regretting having started!"

"Oh, do you mean to wreak vengeance upon me?"

"Have you forgotten how ticklish you are?"

Menace in his voice, he shifted along the bench, wriggling his fingers as if in preparation, that predatory look entering the green eyes.

Marianne laughed, holding up her hands. "I surrender!"

"Faint-heart!"

She let out a giggle, hardly aware how her gaze devoured him, so heartening was it to be at ease with him again.

The green eyes were alight as they stared into hers. Then they changed as some thought entered his mind, and the amusement died out of his face. He got up abruptly, took a couple of steps away from the bench and halted, staring out over the grounds.

Marianne's heart lurched. What had prompted that? Afraid of losing the closeness again, she did not hesitate.

"What is it, Justin? What is amiss?"

He did not turn, but his back stiffened. "Nothing. At least — I just — everything came back." He glanced back over his shoulder. "You teased me into forgetting for a moment, and I thank you for that."

Marianne rose and went to him, setting a hand on his arm. "Don't shut me out, Justin, please. I've missed you so much."

Still he did not turn. Watching his profile, she saw his jaw tense.

"I've missed you too. I thought it better — it wasn't appropriate when…"

His voice died, but Marianne took it up.

"When you were going to be betrothed. Yes, I see that."

She must have allowed her emotions to sound in her voice, for he did turn then, seizing her hand and holding it fast, his gaze intense.

"You didn't deserve it, Marianne. You've been such a good friend to me. But I couldn't — it would have looked —"

"It would have looked unseemly to be so free with another woman."

A flicker of something passed across his face. "You do understand. I should have known you would."

She released herself from his loosened hold, the hurt too fierce to endure his touch. She knew it to be unjustified, but that did nothing to lessen its impact. She spoke in as normal as tone as she could manage. "Well, that's settled then. Shall we turn our attention to what needs to be done?"

"Done?"

His brows had drawn together and she could not read the expression in his eyes.

"About your situation."

"That?" He shook his head a little, as if to clear it. "Yes, I suppose so."

"What sort of reception have you had in the last few days?"

The resumption of the subject did not appear to afford Justin any satisfaction. He looked preoccupied. "I hardly know. Whispers and sly looks. No one has spoken directly."

"Then it is safe to assume the story you have concocted is at least keeping the gossips guessing."

His lip curled. "Hardly. From the pitying glances, I am clearly expected to be broken."

"That must be galling to you."

"It sickens me, if you want the truth."

The hard outer crust was back and regret washed through Marianne. Why could he not have remained easy with her? He was behaving oddly. Not that she'd expected to encounter anything less than anger and hurt pride. But this jerky discomfort, going from one mood to another, was a new Justin and she did not know how to handle him.

"Well, you must show them you are not broken," she said in a bracing tone.

He looked at her. "How? Do you think I'm going to play at gaiety? That would be just as inappropriate."

Marianne's pulse increased as her treacherous heart sent the message coursing into her mind. "You'll have to engage yourself to someone else as quickly as possible."

Justin stared. "Have you run mad?"

She swallowed down her rising apprehension, forcing brightness into her tone. "I am perfectly serious. If you wish to demonstrate your indifference to Selina's elopement, why not?"

He snorted. "All that would get me is the accusation of having taken another woman on the rebound."

"There is that."

"Besides, how in the world am I to find an eligible female in short order? Do you think I'm willing to marry just anyone?"

She remembered his earlier slip and a flurry disturbed her already racing heartbeat. Was he pining for another? "Is there — do you also have a prior attachment?"

"No!" The denial was forceful, almost furious. "What makes you think that?"

"Nothing. I only wondered."

"Well, wonder no longer!"

Despite everything, Marianne's patience failed. "You need not snap my nose off, Justin. I am doing my best to help you."

He was silent, his hands clenching and unclenching at his sides.

Marianne waited a moment, but his jaw was set tight. She knew not what to think. Or whether to believe him. What if she probed more subtly?

"You've already made it clear you require a high-born wife."

"I never said high-born. I said eligible."

"Well-born then."

"That goes without saying." He threw up his hands. "Why are we discussing this? I have no intention of offering for anyone, when I've only just escaped from —"

He broke off, flushing. Marianne eyed him.

"From one unsuitable marriage."

"It wasn't unsuitable."

"How, if neither of you wanted it?"

"In the eyes of Society, I mean."

"And in your father's eyes. Is that what you want, Justin? To marry someone of whom your father would have approved? He's been dead for years."

Justin rolled his eyes. Then, abruptly, he sat down on the bench again and dropped his head in his hands.

Marianne watched him, wrung with distress and exasperation both. Was he determined to waste any chance at happiness on account of his father's rigid views? Left to himself, he would no doubt go off in due course and choose some other obnoxious creature determined upon securing a title merely for the sake of it. What kind of life would he have with one such?

Her heart rose in rebellion. She could make him happy. Oh, she could! If he truly was heart-free, as he claimed. She loved him dearly enough. And she'd been running his household for years. Who better to secure his future?

Except that she lacked the one thing Justin believed he must have in a wife. She was a nobody, born of genteel parents, yes, but of no particular renown. An obscure naval lieutenant, second son of a vicar, and the equally obscure though capable Lavinia, whose only claim to notice was the cousin who had captivated the widowed Earl of Purford, quite by chance when he'd met her at an assembly in Bath.

Marianne was fully alive to the sense of inferiority that plagued Grace, leaving her vulnerable to slights, whether real or imagined, from rival ladies of the *ton*. If, by some miracle, Justin was brought to think of her in the light of a desirable partner for life, Marianne would lay herself open to precisely that kind of disdain.

The awful truth seeped in, killing all hope. Bad enough for her, but worse for Justin. The gossips would have a field day at his expense. No, it could not be done.

Her heart cried out that it should not matter. His happiness was far more important than a parcel of wagging tongues. Only Marianne could not persuade herself it was truly his happiness rather than her own for which she wanted to fight.

Besides, the sneaking suspicion already raised would not be silenced. Despite his vehement denial, perhaps because of it, she could not shake the notion he did cherish an unacknowledged affection. If so, it must be for some wildly unsuitable creature his father would not have approved.

Worse still, if Justin would not think of marrying one he cared for now he was free to choose, there was no earthly hope of his consenting to wed Marianne. She had been crazy to think for a single instant that she had a chance.

The let-down sent a wash of grief coursing through her veins that demanded instant relief.

Somehow she kept her countenance. Somehow she dredged up a tone as close to normality as made no odds. Close enough for Justin, wrapped up in his own agonies, to fail to notice.

"I must go and pack. When do you wish to set forward?"

# Chapter Ten

Would this season never end? While he smiled and played a role as hypocritical as any played by his erstwhile prospective in-laws, Justin writhed and seethed inside. He had thought his situation bad enough before Selina threw her cap over the windmill. Released from that hell, his life had become almost intolerable.

His eyes strayed to where Marianne was standing, a little away from Grace and a coterie of matrons. She seemed to be enjoying a conversation with Alexander. Wasn't that her teasing look? His cousin let out a guffaw and Justin winced.

Come to think of it, had he not seen his cousin approach her at a number of these gatherings? Had he developed a tendre for Marianne? Ha! Aunt Pippa would soon put a stop to that. She could no more wish her son to marry a nobody than his father —

No! There was no use in pursuing that thought. The road was closed years ago.

He had bungled it badly, too deep in his own head to take proper care. He had thought himself long cured, but the sudden taste of freedom had opened a crack which threatened to grow wide and swallow him whole. His desperate attempts to pull the edges back together left him with the feeling of passing through a nightmare.

He did not think he had betrayed himself. Marianne was astute, but by the time they had set forth, he'd had himself well in hand.

When he had gone, at her request, to look over the work done in the rooms meant for Selina, he had almost lost that iron control. The transformation in the bedchamber, with Marianne standing there just as if she belonged, very nearly undid him. It was almost as if she had created the place with herself in mind, it suited so well with her personality. But that was nonsense, thank God. She'd made that clear at once, indicating the hangings.

"I'm afraid this was the best of what Petherick had to offer. It is perhaps a trifle frivolous for Lady Selina, but I thought it was pretty and it does make the room brighter."

He agreed to it, adding his thanks for all she'd done.

"Don't thank me. But I do want you to make a point of thanking the sewing women and the estate carpenters, all the workers in fact. I've asked Sprake to assemble everyone who had a hand in the work in the hall this afternoon."

He balked. "What, and thank them for wasting their time?"

Marianne's tone became minatory. "Justin, they've slaved hours every day for three weeks to get it ready in time. It's not their fault Lady Selina chose to run away."

Her words shot him through with guilt and his cheeks warmed. "Of course not. I'll say everything that is appropriate."

"I'm sorry for it, but you will have to explain the circumstances."

Her insistence galled him. "As if the news has not by this time filtered down to the lowest menial and travelled half across the county."

Marianne was, just as he might have expected, inexorable. "That's as may be. You can't avoid mentioning the matter, since they need to understand why their efforts have been in vain."

She was right, as usual. He'd been daunted by the sea of sympathetic faces, clearly taking him for an object of pity, but he hoped he had come the earl satisfactorily.

Due solely to Marianne's ease of manner, the hours together in his phaeton passed in relative amity, with no dangerous subjects arising since Laxey was up behind and would hear every word. He'd feared a tête-à-tête and was relieved when she had elected to accompany him in this vehicle.

"Go in the stuffy coach when you have driven yourself down? No, indeed, Justin. Besides, we'll be a deal quicker and I've only the one portmanteau."

The necessity to mind his horses allowed him to spend much of the time in silence. Marianne knew better than to chatter when his attention was engaged. Besides, she was never one to waste words in idle conversation. It was one of the things he liked in her.

She was also dependable, capable, trustworthy, kind, considerate and honest. Too much so upon occasion. She might not be a beauty, but she had countenance and that rich chestnut hair he'd run his fingers through that time she took a tumble when they were out riding and her bonnet fell off. Marianne had not been much hurt beyond a few bruises, but her hair had come down and Justin had tidied it.

He remembered her smiling up at him as he did so, and how he'd very nearly lost his head and kissed her there and then.

"Justin, have you forgotten I am promised to you for the next dance?"

The anxious voice cut thankfully into the memory. He forced a smile.

"My dear little sister, how could I possibly forget?"

"Well, you were looking like a moonling with your head in the clouds."

Jocasta was nothing if not forthright. He steered her towards the couples taking their places in the set. A flicker of pride ran through him. She looked delightful, gowned of course in the ubiquitous white muslin of present fashion. The short sleeves were full and frilled with lace and a lace ruff stood up behind. Some sort of purple drapery went about the shoulders and in a flow of loops to the floor.

"You look decidedly elegant, little sister."

She flushed prettily. "Elegant? Pooh!"

"A pity the elegance does not extend to your language."

Jocasta laughed at his stricture, and no more was said until they passed in the movement of the dance.

"You've got to stand up with other girls, Justin."

He waited until she joined him again, his eyes on the second couple taking their turn in the centre. "I'm not going to afford the gossips more food for talk, Jocasta."

"They're talking now because you don't."

He frowned down at her. "How do you know?"

She cast him a scornful glance. "Delia told me, of course. How do you think?"

Irritation swept through him. "I could wish your friend would be a little less busy."

Jocasta's giggle sounded, but he was obliged to wait to ask the reason until the end of the next figure. But when they were still again, his sister volunteered it.

"Are you blind, Justin? Delia is setting her cap at you."

"Oh my God!"

"As would a dozen other girls if you cared to notice them."

"For pity's sake! What am I, a prize bull?"

"You're an earl, stupid! And you're available again."

Exasperation seized him, but he was obliged to express it in a savage murmur. "First I'm an object of pity and now I'm a target for matchmakers. Why in the world should anyone suppose I'm interested after —?"

"They don't suppose it," said his newly worldly-wise sister, "but that won't stop them having a touch at you."

Seething all over again, Justin took her hand for their turn in the centre, performing the steps automatically as he scanned a scattering of female faces round about. Jocasta's giggle exacerbated his temper.

"It's no use you glaring, Justin. That won't stop them."

"Then what will?"

"Nothing. At least, not until you offer for someone else."

"I've no intention of offering for anyone else."

"You'll have to eventually. You can't remain single forever. What about your heir?"

He was never more glad to hear the final notes of the music. He bowed formally, giving his sister a look as he did so that boded her no good at all. To his chagrin, she smiled brightly up at him and leaned a little closer to whisper.

"Stand up with someone else or be doomed, big brother!"

With difficulty, he suppressed a retort. In honour bound, he offered his arm and Jocasta tucked her hand into it. "Who is your next victim?"

She bubbled over. "I'm so glad you're not stuffy, Justin. Imagine if I had a guardian as strict and horrid as the Dragon."

"If you're not careful, you may find yourself with just such a guardian."

"Pooh! You can't change now. Mama says you've spoiled me to death, which I can't deny, and —"

"And I'm reaping the consequences. I thank you, I had already realised that for myself."

Despite the annoyance engendered by her disclosures, her infectious laughter could not but melt him. He steered her towards Grace. "The one consolation I have is that you're bound to be off my hands in short order, since I see a veritable queue of suitors waiting for you."

"Yes, is it not amusing? I thought I should be quite shunned with the scandal, but instead I have acquired a respectable court."

Justin halted, turning to look down at her in some surprise. "Are you serious?"

Her mischievous look appeared and it struck him that his little sister was in unexpectedly good spirits.

"Odd, is it not, that your misfortune has brought me into notice? If it had not overset you so much, I'd be over the moon."

His heart swelled and he set his hand over hers where it lay on his arm and pressed it. "Be over the moon, my lovely. I'm delighted for you and I wish I'd taken time to see it for myself."

"Oh, tush! You've had quite enough to worry you, and you need not think I feel hardly used, for I don't."

He had to laugh. "I can see that. You're in high croak and no wonder."

Turning again, he led her through the press of persons, trying as he did so to identify the various gentlemen waiting for her return.

"Do you favour any of them, Jocasta?"

"None more than another."

"Well, you need be in no hurry to choose."

"I thought you were eager to be rid of me."

He raised his brows. "I am, of course, but not at the expense of your happiness."

Jocasta's eyes rimmed with moisture and her cheeks grew pink. "Oh, Justin, I do love you, best of brothers! And I do wish you —" She broke off, flushing more deeply still.

"You wish what?"

"Nothing. I forget what I was going to say."

"No, you didn't."

"Well, it's not important."

"Then why did it put you to the blush?"

Jocasta fidgeted, looking away. Then she withdrew her hand. "Oh, look, Tazewell is waiting for me. He has the next dance."

With that, she darted away, flitting so swiftly through the intervening couples he had no chance to catch her. He watched her join young Lord Tazewell, who greeted her with enthusiasm and immediately led her towards the floor where the next sets were beginning to form.

Justin was left with an unanswered question and a raft of conjecture. He was just resolving to tackle Jocasta at the first opportunity when he was hailed by his cousin.

"Care for a breather, old fellow? I'm parched. Shall we go in search of refreshments?"

A sigh escaped Justin. Just the excuse he needed. "Nothing would give me greater pleasure."

Lord Dymond, whose tall figure admirably set off the current vogue for well-fitting breeches and square-tailed coats, gave him a sympathetic look as they headed out of the ballroom. "Finding the going rough?"

"You have no idea, Alex. And my sister, if you please, informs me that I have now become a target for matchmakers."

"Should think you might. Never lose an opportunity, those tabbies."

"I've a good mind to put a sign round my neck saying I'm not for sale."

His cousin gave a bark of laughter and clapped him on the back. "No need, coz. That Friday Face you've been wearing is enough to tell 'em so."

A jolt shot through Justin. Had he been so obvious? If so, it was the last thing he'd intended, besides being impolitic. Uncivil too.

They had arrived by this time in a saloon where refreshments were laid out, and Alex headed for a servant in charge of the liquor.

"Claret, old fellow?"

He handed Justin a glass, at which he sipped, feeling a measure of relief as the wine warmed his throat.

"What's to do, coz? Still pipped at the gossip? My mother thinks it's died down a trifle."

Justin sought for words to express the emotions that dogged him, without wholly giving himself away. "I am a trifle blue-devilled."

"Not surprised. Enough to throw anyone into the dismals."

Alex threw the wine down his throat and held out his glass for a refill. He nodded at Justin's nearly full glass. "Get that down you, dear boy. Put some heart into you."

Justin tossed off the rest of the wine and did indeed feel better. His cousin took the glass and returned it to him with another measure of the red liquid inside. Then he steered Justin to a clear space where they might be relatively private, since there were only a few knots of guests in the room.

Wondering what was coming, Justin gave him an enquiring look.

Alex grinned. "Only going to ask what you intend to do, coz. Do you mean to remain 'til the season's over?"

Justin sighed. "I must, for Jocasta's sake. She would be wild with me if I sought an early return to Purford Park. She's having the time of her life, it seems."

His cousin laughed. "Turned into a regular belle. Marianne was saying she's coming into her own."

Justin's breath tightened as he recalled his earlier suspicion of Alex's interest in Marianne. He took a sip of wine to fortify himself and spoke in as casual a tone as he could muster. "Yes, she's been so cribbed by Grace and the Dragon, it was a question whether Jocasta's natural vivacity would be crushed."

"Not she! It'd take a hammer to crush that sister of yours. Bad as Georgy."

A spontaneous laugh escaped Justin. "Yes, I recall several occasions when your little sister and mine together were like to drive us all demented. Jocasta can be quite a handful. Grace will have it that I've spoiled her."

"Marianne don't think so. Says you've been the best brother a girl could hope for. And she should know."

A sliver of something unfathomable touched Justin's core. "Meaning?"

Alex's brows rose. "Wasn't being cryptic, coz. Ain't you and Marianne been like brother and sister? Always seemed so to me."

It was so. Or should have been. Though he'd never treated Marianne the way he treated Jocasta. "We are more friends than siblings."

"Understandable. She's a deal older than Jocasta."

It had nothing to do with age, but Justin did not say so. Instead he eyed his cousin, conscious of a faint hostility in himself.

"You seem to be becoming just as friendly with Marianne."

Alex's barking laughter rang out. "Don't be a nodcock, coz. Don't know her near as well as you do. Mind, I like her. Always have."

Justin set his teeth. "How much?"

His cousin blinked. "How much what?"

"How much do you like Marianne?"

A frown creased Lord Dymond's forehead. "What's to do? You can't have shot the cat, you ain't had enough. Unless you've been knocking back the claret all evening?"

"I have not."

"Then what in Hades is making you bristle like this? Know you're edgy, old fellow, but no need to come the ugly with me."

With difficulty, Justin suppressed the unprecedented rise of rage. "I beg your pardon, cousin."

Alex eyed him. "You might well. What's got into you?"

Taking refuge in his glass, Justin strove for control. But the suspicion would not be contained. "Are you dangling after Marianne, Alex?"

His cousin's brow cleared. "Ah, I see what it is." His laugh was hearty. "Behaving just like a brother, ain't you? No, of course I'm not. My mother gave me the office."

Relief was instantly followed by anxiety. "What office?"

"Thinks Marianne ought to be leg-shackled. Told me to hang about her in hopes of bringing her into notice."

"So other men might take interest?"

"That's it. Downy one, my mother. Knows fellows always start sniffing about if they think there's something to see. Says men are like dogs."

Amusement crept through Justin's annoyance. "I can almost hear Aunt Pippa saying it." The inevitable query raised its head. "And are they? Sniffing round Marianne, I mean?"

"Lord, yes. Ain't you noticed?"

He had not. Granted, he'd seen her talking with animation, but he'd looked only at Marianne, not at who she was with. Except for Alex. She was always easy and conversable in company. Could it be true that she was sought after?

"I've not seen her dancing."

Alex looked regretful. "Marianne won't dance. Insists she's a chaperon and it wouldn't suit. Besides, says she's so out of practice, she's forgotten the figures."

"Nonsense, she can't have forgotten. She was helping Jocasta practice last year."

"If that's so, perhaps she don't enjoy dancing."

Remembering earlier years, Justin spoke without thinking. "That's ridiculous. She loves to dance."

"Well, try if you can persuade her, old fellow, for I've had no luck at all."

Panic swept through Justin. "No! No, I can't." He sought for a valid excuse. "Except for doing my duty by Jocasta, I'm staying off the floor. Especially after what she's told me. If I favour one female, I'll be expected to dance with others."

"Oh, you'd get away with it with Marianne. Everyone knows she's family."

# Chapter Eleven

The end of the season could not come soon enough for Marianne. If it was not for Grace, she would have found an excuse to return to Purford Park. But her cousin had been so knocked back by the shocking manner of the breach of Justin's engagement she would not venture into company without Marianne's support.

"I can't and won't face any of those hateful wretches if you are not by, Marianne. I only have to see that Guineaford creature to feel utterly crushed."

In reality, once she was engaged with her particular friends, Marianne had only to keep within sight. And since Jocasta had found her feet, she had leisure to amuse herself, if she'd a mind to do so. But she had not.

The few morning visits they were obliged to make were not so bad, but every evening party was torture. If Justin was present, she could not drag her attention away from him. If he was absent, she was restless and unable to prevent herself wondering where he was and what he might be doing.

The hideous fear he would be snatched up by some designing female haunted her dreams. Jocasta was driving her crazy with a barrage of speculation.

"I've never seen Delia so determined. And she's not the only one. It's quite a comedy to see how they weave a path to put themselves in his way, only to be confounded when Justin refuses to notice."

Which was Marianne's only solace. It was obvious to the meanest intelligence that Justin was smarting still. It hurt to see the distress he was struggling to conceal, without much success. She longed to offer comfort, but found it so hard to be natural with him she was apt to steer clear of anything resembling a tête-à-tête.

As if all this was not bad enough, Lady Luthrie must needs take it into her head to promote her scheme for Marianne's future.

The matron had caught her alone a few days after her return.

"I came to see how Grace did, but I am glad to have a moment with you, Marianne."

After an energetic discussion about Grace's deportment in public, when Marianne was able to assure the matron she had been persuaded to do her part in scotching the scandal, she was both chagrined and dismayed to find herself the subject of Lady Luthrie's managing disposition.

"I am glad you are obliged to accompany Grace. Nothing could be better. It will provide you with the perfect excuse to look about you."

So far from her thoughts had it been to think of a future other than one with Justin, Marianne did not at first comprehend her meaning.

"Look about me for what, ma'am?"

"Why, a prospective husband, of course. Have I not been saying how necessary it is that you should dispose of yourself suitably?"

Marianne balked. "You said it once, ma'am. Moreover, it is hardly the moment for me to be thinking of myself."

"On the contrary, it is exactly the moment. If Jocasta should contract an engagement, it is highly unlikely Grace will come to Town next season. And once Justin finds a replacement for Lady Selina —"

"He shows no disposition to be in a hurry to do that," Marianne cut in, the very thought pricking at her deepest wound.

"But he must marry in due course, or have an obscure cousin inherit. He will have his pick of the eligibles, and you may be sure a pack of hopefuls will be thrust at him."

"They already are, according to Jocasta."

"Well, there you are. He will not resist forever, and you ought to be just as determined as any of them."

If only she had the courage! Except Lady Luthrie did not mean for her to set her cap at Justin.

"For a start, you must gown yourself with more appeal, my dear. Not that I dislike that blue gown on you, but coloured muslins are quite out since the century turned. There is no need to go about looking like an ape-leader."

"I am an ape-leader, Lady Luthrie. I'm almost five and twenty."

"Young enough to make a suitable wife."

"For whom, ma'am?"

"Why, almost anyone, if you will but smarten yourself up a little. A fresh look will do wonders."

Marianne was about to repudiate the suggestion when Lady Luthrie threw her into shock.

"I dare say you would prefer not to be beholden to your cousin, my dear, so I propose to gown you myself."

"You cannot mean it!"

Lady Luthrie's beak of a nose was lifted. "Why can I not? I am not without experience. I've gowned two daughters, I'll have you know. Besides, it would give me pleasure."

"But I can't possibly accept such generosity, ma'am. It is extremely kind of you and I am grateful, but it would not do. It would be a waste besides, for such a short period of time."

Lady Luthrie looked regretful. "I suppose that is true. At least promise me you will think of yourself rather than devoting your whole attention to Grace."

It was easy enough to reassure the matron since Marianne's attention was in fact taken up with Justin. When she found Lady Luthrie's son dancing attendance on her, she was rather amused than otherwise. She liked Lord Dymond's easy manners and had always found him entertaining. Nevertheless, she taxed him with having been egged on by Lady Luthrie.

"Are you your mother's deputy then, Alex? Do you mean to try and persuade me into looking about me for a husband?"

Alex's guffaw had made her smile.

"You're nothing if not shrewd, Marianne. To tell you true, my mother thought it'd break the ice so you'd not be ranged with the chaperons."

"It's too late for that, Alex. Not that I object to your company."

"Nor I yours. Always fond of you, Marianne. Happy to be of service. Will you dance with me?"

But nothing he could say would make Marianne break her habit of propriety. She had no wish to bring further gossip on the family, and she was well aware her cousin's acquaintance thought of her as Grace's companion, or her deputy in chaperoning Jocasta. To behave otherwise would bring down censure upon all their heads.

She was not prepared for Justin's sudden descent upon her, however. She had just ensured Jocasta was fully occupied and was hovering near Grace, who was engaged in animated conversation with Lady Burloyne, when he spoke directly behind her.

"Marianne, I need you!"

Her heart jerked and she turned so swiftly she almost lost her balance.

Justin reached out a hand to aid her, a rueful look crossing his face. "Steady! Did I startle you? I beg your pardon."

A fluttery laugh escaped her and she was glad of a valid excuse for her trembling hands. "You took me off guard. What's to do?"

He released her arm and a faint grin lightened the gloom he'd been wearing. "You have to dance with me."

Marianne's mind went blank. "Dance with you?"

"Yes, you birdwit. You know, join a set and twirl about the floor? You've heard of dancing, I presume?"

She broke into laughter, warmth spreading through her veins. "Indeed I have, but as you well know, I do not indulge."

"You do with me. Or at least you will."

"Will I? Why is that?"

"Because Jocasta says I must dance or be doomed and you're the only woman who won't immediately assume I'm ready to lay my heart at her feet."

As if she had ever dared to assume any such thing! He had spoken in the light teasing way she knew and loved, but the strain was visible in his eyes. An effort she understood, for she was under just the same pressure. Her heart ached for him all over again and she spoke with real regret. "Justin, I can't."

His smile was a trifle awry. "Yes, I know you range yourself with the tabbies past the age of dancing, but this is me, Marianne."

An even more telling reason why she should not break her own rule. How could she dance with Justin and not give herself away?

"Exactly so. It would look too particular."

"Good God, what does that matter?" Impatience was in both face and voice. "People are bound to talk whatever I do."

"But not about me." An arrested look took the place of impatience and Marianne drove the message home. "As long as I remain the shadow in the background, I excite no undue interest. If I'm seen dancing — especially with you — I will be held to be putting myself forward unbecomingly."

And thought to be setting her cap at him like all the other wretches who were plotting to steal him from her. But this she kept to herself.

He was frowning. "Why especially with me?"

"Now who is being a birdwit? Because you are an object of considerable interest already."

The frown did not abate. "I don't see that at all. All anyone would think is I'm only willing to dance with females of the family. And they'd be right."

"Then why dance at all? Other than with Jocasta, I mean."

Mischief flitted across his face. "Truth? Alex challenged me to succeed where he failed."

The fluttery feeling returned at the thought he'd been discussing her and she gave a shaky laugh. "Wretch! If you think I'm going to win your wager for you, think again."

"It wasn't a wager, merely a cousinly dare."

"Well, whatever it was, you will be obliged to go back and report failure."

He leaned a little closer, the teasing glint pronounced. "If we weren't in public, I'd be tempted to tickle you into submission."

Marianne took an involuntary step back as her heart gave a sudden thud. She struggled to keep the treacherous rise of anticipation out of her face.

"You wouldn't dare!"

"Oh, wouldn't I?"

"Justin, behave! You're embarrassing me."

She'd spoken in an urgent under-voice and he jerked upright, looking quickly around. Had he forgotten where they were for a moment?

His smile looked mechanical as the erstwhile trouble crept back into his countenance. Marianne's heart dipped. Impelled, she uttered fatal words.

"Very well, I'll dance with you."

Justin's eyes lit and a flush of heat shot through her. In a dim part of her mind, common sense made frantic passes in a bid to reassert its authority. But Marianne's dreams swam too giddily to respond. She gave her hand into Justin's and allowed him to lead her into one of the sets then forming, oblivious for a brief moment to her surroundings.

When she took her place next to Justin in the square of four couples, however, she came to her senses in a bang. What in the world was she doing? The female of the couple opposite was staring in a fashion as insolent as it was curious. A quick glance about sufficed to tell Marianne she was not the only one.

Thus exposed, she felt all the force of Lady Luthrie's comments upon her gowns, convinced the striped silk gauze petticoat and scarlet polonaise she'd hitherto thought pretty, made her look dowdy instead.

An abrupt sensation of being trapped possessed her. Wild ideas of escape screamed through her mind, even to pretending a swoon.

Too late! The musicians struck up and the dance began.

Justin kept up a flow of remarks whenever the figure brought them together, but Marianne answered him at random. It was purgatory to be unable to take pleasure in being where she'd longed to be, partnered at his side with his smile and his touch directed only at her. Aware throughout of envious or disapproving female faces, she moved through the motions of the dance with all the grace of an automaton. She certainly felt like one, barely able to recall which way she must turn next, and grateful for Justin's guiding hand. She had to make an especial effort not to cling to his fingers as he took her hand for the ronde.

As the last note sounded, she sighed with relief and sank into her curtsy on the final chords.

As she took Justin's proffered arm to lead her off the floor, a low murmur reached her. "Forgive me, Marianne. That was ill-advised."

"It's too late now for regret. The damage is done." She felt him stiffen beside her and at once regretted the tart note. She tried to backtrack. "Never mind it. I dare say I shall survive."

There was time for no more. Lady Luthrie loomed up before her.

"Excellently done, Justin. A very good beginning. Now you must dance with Alexander, Marianne."

Aware of Justin's frowning stare, Marianne spoke in a lowered tone. "I doubt I could endure it, ma'am."

She came under fire from the matron's beaky nose.

"Nonsense, my girl! Are you afraid of a parcel of busybodies?"

"For pity's sake, Aunt Pippa, let her alone!"

Lady Luthrie's masterful eye turned on her nephew. "This does not concern you, my dear Justin. You've done your part. And a very good thing you've taken to the floor with someone other than your sister. Now you may gratify some other young lady with a turn."

Justin's face of baffled fury threw Marianne into a desire to dissolve into hysterical giggles. She was obliged to exercise severe self-control to suppress it, which at least served to pull her back into a semblance of her customary calm.

Before she could say anything, however, Alex appeared. Oblivious to the prevailing mood, he clapped his cousin on the back.

"My compliments, old fellow! Said you'd do it and you did. My turn now, Marianne."

"I don't —"

"Now don't say you won't stand up with me, for I'll take it in snuff. Dashed insulting to refuse me after you've danced with my coz."

Marianne was left with nothing to say. A glance at Justin found him tight-lipped, a smoulder at his eyes.

"Quite right, Alexander," approved his mother, ignoring her nephew altogether. "Off with you, Marianne."

"But Grace — Jocasta—"

"Neither needs you at this moment. See, people are taking their places. Now, go."

Since Alex was steering her back onto the floor, Marianne had little choice. One could not cause a scene by refusing to enter the set. That would make tongues wag even more.

As she took her place, she caught sight of Grace's face, directed upon her in an expression of blank astonishment. Dismay flooded through her. How in the world was she to explain?

The evening began to assume the aspect of a nightmare.

# Chapter Twelve

A simmering atmosphere over the breakfast cups did nothing to settle Justin's disordered senses. Since such talk as was embarked upon centred in an oblique fashion on the events of the previous night, he was glad of the presence of the servants.

Marianne was looking pale and was, he guessed, as discomposed as he. She appeared calm on the surface, but regarding her narrowly, Justin detected a tell-tale quiver in her cheek and a hunted look in her eyes.

For the rest, Jocasta was gleeful, the Dragon bewildered and Grace sullen. He was tempted to demand the reason, but shrank from precipitating a scene. It was evident there had been words between his stepmother and Marianne. They were avoiding each other's eyes and Grace addressed her remarks in the main to Miss Stubbings, who had been absent from Lady Colgrave's ball.

He'd been informed by his sister that since Jocasta was firmly established, and both Grace and Marianne were at hand, the Dragon was unnecessary. He had refused her request to turn the creature off, however.

"She might have outlived her usefulness to you, my dear sister, but one can't throw an elderly governess out at a moment's notice. She must be given adequate time to find another post — if she can at her age."

"That's what Marianne says, but I wish you would at least tell her I am no longer under her jurisdiction."

This he had refused to do, on the score that if Grace was ill and Marianne occupied, she might still be required to chaperon her charge.

Her presence this morning was proving useful, since it prevented Jocasta's more outrageous utterances. She was too used to being under her preceptress's thumb to break the habit of minding her tongue in the woman's presence.

Justin was inclined to lay the blame at his aunt's door. But for her intervention, his ill-fated dance with Marianne would have been the sum of it. Alex would not have taken his turn with her, and the devil on his shoulder would not have urged him to carry out Aunt Pippa's suggestion he favour some other female.

Not that he'd done it at her behest. The sight of Marianne being squired by his cousin had galled him. He'd looked around for the nearest available female and found Delia Burloyne almost at his elbow. She had been only too willing to oblige him, her face lighting up in a way that brought his senses crashing back. Too late he realised he was raising expectations. Exactly what he'd taken care not to do. As he and his partner joined the last set being formed, he'd known he must lead out at least two more debutantes in order to damp any notion of his having singled Delia out.

He finished his repast with a sense of relief and rose from the table.

Grace cast him a look of reproach. "I hope you do not mean to go out, Justin. I would like a word, if you please."

Nothing could please him less, but he could hardly say so. Aware of Jocasta's gaze, brimful of mischief, he flicked a glance at Marianne and found her staring at the coffee cup held between her hands.

"Certainly, ma'am. Shall we go into the morning room?"

Grace got up, swishing to the door in her round morning dress of imperial pale blue silk, but before he could lead her out of the room, the door opened and his aunt walked in.

"Ah, I am glad you are all still here. I came on purpose to catch you."

Grace was positively glaring. "Philippa! What brings you here, I should like to know?"

His aunt raised her brows at the peevish tone, but made no answer. Her gimlet gaze swept to the butler. "You may give me a cup of coffee, Rowsham. And then leave us, if you please."

Wholly ignoring Grace's face of chagrin, she then sailed to the chair Simon set for her next to Marianne, her magnificent pelisse of scarlet velvet swirling as she sat.

Faint amusement lightened Justin's sombre mood. Typical of Aunt Pippa to assume authority in his house, usurping both himself and Grace. He knew Rowsham would not stir from the room until he received assent from his master.

Justin therefore resumed his seat, took another cup of coffee for himself and then nodded dismissal. He turned to his aunt as the door closed behind the butler and footman.

"A family conference, Aunt Pippa?"

"Something of the sort."

She looked across the table at the Dragon as she spoke. Formidable as she herself was, Miss Stubbings was no match for Lady Luthrie. She rose.

"I will leave you, dear Lady Purford."

"Stay where you are, Amelia," said Grace, in an unusual attempt to resume control. "If you are come to talk of last night, Philippa, it will be as well for Miss Stubbings to be fully acquainted with the matter. My health has suffered and I cannot guarantee to be well enough to take Jocasta about."

Justin cast a look at Marianne, but she did not raise her eyes from her cup. It struck him that her fingers were rigid. His aunt was eyeing him, clearly in the expectation he would send the Dragon away. But ruffling Grace's feathers would serve no useful purpose.

"Do sit down again, Miss Stubbings."

Jocasta gave him a dagger look, which he ignored. He turned his attention to his masterful relative. "Well, Aunt?"

She gave a snort, gazing about the table from under the scarlet cap, trimmed with sable like the coat. "It is just as I suspected. An excellent turn has been relegated to the status of a tragedy, I perceive."

Her eyes turned on Grace as she spoke. His stepmother flushed, the glare at her eyes increasing.

"Excellent? Pray how is it excellent, when Justin and Marianne between them have set the whole Town talking again?"

Marianne looked up at last. "I have apologised over and over again, cousin. I would I might undo it, but I cannot."

Her tone, both weary and dejected, threw Justin back into disorder. He wished the rest of the room at Jericho, but his aunt took up the gage at once.

"Undo it? I should rather think not. My dear Grace, I cannot imagine why you are taking up this nonsensical attitude. Justin has shown himself to be back on the market."

"Have I indeed?"

"Yes, you have, big brother, and a very good thing too. I'm so glad you took my advice."

"Jocasta! Do you mean to say this is your fault? How dared you interfere?"

"Come down off your high ropes, Grace, for heaven's sake," cut in Lady Luthrie. "If Jocasta had the sense to urge her brother to behave like a normal man, she has a deal more common sense than I had supposed."

Grace's features grew more flushed and she eyed her sister-in-law with deep reproach. "I suppose you mean to imply that I have none?"

His aunt's brows rose again. "Did I say so? Believe me, I fully comprehend your feelings, but you are mistaken in your ideas, my dear Grace."

"What do you mean?"

"You suppose harm to have been done by Justin having danced with Marianne, do you not?"

Justin would have intervened at this point to spare Marianne's feelings, but Grace exploded.

"Of course there was harm! No fewer than three persons hinted to me how shocking they thought it for Marianne to be putting herself forward in such a way."

"Three idiots, you mean."

Justin had to bite down on a laugh, but he felt obliged to cut in. "Aunt, you are distressing Grace."

"Well, I am sorry, but it must be said."

Grace's face puckered and Justin inwardly groaned. Not tears, for pity's sake!

"How can you be so unkind, Philippa? As if my nerves were not already overset."

The Dragon, tutting as she cast a glance of dislike at the perpetrator, rose and went to her, patting her on the shoulder.

"This is turning into a farce," Jocasta muttered and Justin found himself the recipient of a comical grimace.

He was about to call a halt to the proceedings when Marianne suddenly stood up.

"I must beg to be excused."

Justin got up quickly as she moved towards the door, but his aunt's voice arrested her.

"Sit down, Marianne, if you please. There is nothing to be gained by running off. Moreover, it is scarcely conduct I expected from you."

Marianne turned at the door, a look of anguish in her eyes. "I have already surpassed the conduct expected from me. This will make little difference."

"Don't be ridiculous. Come here, girl, and sit back down."

Grace reared up. "You need not bring her back on my account. She has utterly betrayed me!"

Justin could not let this pass. "Grace, that is unfair! If you must blame anyone, blame me. Marianne did her utmost to resist. It was I who insisted on her dancing."

"Then you did very wrong. I would not have thought it of you, Justin."

"Upon my word, Grace! You ought to be upon the stage!"

The effect of Lady Luthrie's pronouncement could not but bear out Jocasta's stigmatising the scene as a farce. She succumbed to a fit of the giggles. Grace gave a shriek of rage and threw herself into the Dragon's willing arms, where she broke into sobs while Miss Stubbings tutted over her head, casting unloving glances at the author of the outrage. Only Marianne remained unmoved, still standing rigidly by the door.

Obeying his instinct, Justin crossed the room to her side and took one stiff hand in his. "Don't heed her, Marianne. She'll come about."

"If only I might go to my room."

"It will only prolong the agony. Come. Sit down."

He obliged her to return to the table and resume her seat. Before going back to his own, he approached Grace's chair. "Please try to control yourself, Grace. We will get nowhere unless we can all remain calm."

Grace raised her head from where it rested on the Dragon's bosom. "Calm? When I have been insulted in my own home?"

Justin gave his aunt an admonitory look. She threw up her eyes, but nevertheless capitulated.

"Accept my apologies, Grace. I spoke in the heat of the moment."

Grace sniffed at the vinaigrette which had miraculously appeared in her fingers, and consented to be appeased. "Very well."

Silence reigned while Justin went back to his chair. He was tempted to ring for Rowsham and demand some more stimulating refreshment than coffee, but that would merely delay things and he wished the scene to be over as swiftly as possible. Consequently he addressed his aunt the moment he sat down again.

"Now that we have the preliminaries out of the way, what is it you really came to say, Aunt Pippa?"

She gave a bark of laughter. "You are not quite the fool I took you for, Purford."

"I thank you. Well?"

"If you must have it, I came to champion Marianne."

"Me? Why, Lady Luthrie?"

"Because, as you very well know, I am persuaded it is time for you to be thinking of your future."

She looked at Grace as she spoke, and Justin noted his stepmother's shocked incomprehension.

"What in the world are you talking of, Philippa? What future?"

"It is high time Marianne found herself a husband."

Justin saw the colour leap into Marianne's face and she broke into hasty speech.

111

"You need not look like that, Cousin Grace. It is none of my doing. I had no thought of such a thing."

"Until I put it into her head."

"Not even then," Marianne argued. "I have no desire to find a husband."

Relief surged into Grace's features and her voice echoed it. "No, indeed. What can you mean by it, Philippa? I could not do without Marianne. How should I manage?"

The selfishness of this response struck at Justin and he had difficulty keeping his tongue between his teeth. His own feelings about the possibility of Marianne marrying notwithstanding, he was disgusted with his stepmother's egotism. So, it was clear, was his aunt.

"My dear Grace, the matter should have been looked to years since."

"Are you mad? Marianne never once expressed a desire to marry."

"Why would she, thinking herself but a poor relation?"

Impatience was once again rife in Lady Luthrie's voice and Justin hoped she was not going to set Grace off again. But Marianne took a hand.

"That is untrue, ma'am. I've never been treated as other than one of the family."

Grace lifted her chin. "You see. Next you will say I made a drudge of her."

"I don't say that, but you will scarcely deny you made use of her services."

Grace gasped, but again Marianne intervened.

"You must not blame my cousin for that, Lady Luthrie. I took on whatever tasks I do for her without the least encouragement."

"Yes, you did, Marianne. I never expected you to do any of it. Not that I'm not grateful, for I am. In my precarious state of health, I have been only too glad of your assistance."

Justin could not forbear a smile, but his aunt's next speech rapidly wiped out his amusement.

"Marianne virtually runs the household, Grace, which is exactly why she must be provided with her own establishment. Since the fiasco with Lady Selina, the matter is no longer urgent, but all the more reason to waste no time. Once Justin is wed, Marianne must give up the reins."

"But she will come with me to the Dower House. She has no need to be seeking a husband."

"The poor girl will be bored rigid."

"I can speak for myself, Lady Luthrie, and I will not be bored."

"Nonsense! You cannot go from running Purford Park to the Dower House and not be moped to death."

"I think it is a splendid notion," said Jocasta, entering the lists. "Marianne ought to be married. She'd make a perfect wife and mother."

A strangled laugh escaped Marianne and Justin was torn between warmth and dismay.

"I thank you, Jocasta, but the matter is not open for debate. I have no wish to marry anyone."

"There, you see, Philippa! Now own yourself mistaken."

"I shall do no such thing. The girl does not know what is good for her, and I am determined to pursue this course. As for help and companionship, which you seem to feel you need, you have Miss Stubbings there, who will make an excellent substitute for Marianne when you are obliged to take up your residence in the Dower House."

Justin could not but applaud this suggestion, which at once satisfied Grace's need and the vexed question of what to do about the Dragon. Except that it left Marianne adrift.

No one cared to comment, it seemed, and Justin had little difficulty in divining their reasons. Setting aside Marianne, it was obvious Grace did not relish the prospect of living only with Miss Stubbings, and Jocasta would only be satisfied with her departure from the family altogether. The Dragon herself had turned a trifle pink. When Grace said nothing, she left her to resume her chair with a meek and dejected air that could not but strike at Justin.

"For once, Aunt Pippa, I am in agreement with you. I had been hoping Miss Stubbings would consent to remain with us, even when Jocasta is wed, whenever that may be. Grace will, I know, be happy to have your company, Miss Stubbings."

The elderly dame threw him such a look of gratitude that he was a trifle embarrassed, since his true sentiments were scarcely in accord with his words.

Grace regarded him with a frown, and then seemed to pull herself together. She turned to the Dragon. "I certainly could not do without you, Amelia. You have been a rock in these dreadful days."

Miss Stubbings disclaimed, but nevertheless looked gratified.

"Now we have that settled," said his aunt, "let us turn our attention to your affairs, Purford."

Only by a supreme effort of will did Marianne refrain from leaping from her seat once again and running out of the breakfast parlour. Bad enough to have to endure a discussion of her potential future. To listen to Lady Luthrie outlining Justin's could only serve to increase the suppressed agitation under which she laboured.

Following the row with Grace, the night had been hideous with unquiet dreams through the little time she managed to sleep at all. She'd never before known her cousin to give herself over to hysterical rage. Even now she was hard put to it to recognise what had prompted the outburst. Was there some underlying fear? Of loneliness perhaps?

Her thoughts were feverish, but she was not permitted to indulge them in the face of Lady Luthrie's determination.

"I have made it my business to discover the extent of the damage caused by your erstwhile betrothed, my dear Justin."

He did not look to be gratified. The reverse rather, for Marianne noted a familiar spark in his eye.

"Have you indeed, Aunt? How?"

Lady Luthrie looked a trifle smug. "I have my sources. Besides, Lady Sessay and I are old friends."

"Yes, I am aware."

An edge to Justin's voice caught Marianne's attention. Did he know then that his aunt had been instrumental in the making of the match? Grace had told Marianne as much when she'd delivered the blow in the first place years ago. Typically, his aunt picked it up.

"You need not look askance, my dear boy. I knew nothing of Selina's preferences, and she was besides a child at the time."

"I am aware of that too."

"Well, that is all beside the bridge and we must concentrate on the present."

At this point, Grace cut in. "What in the world are you at, Philippa? We all know the consequences of that wretched creature's actions. And you, all of you, insisted upon my remaining in Town to endure the slights. I was never more mortified!"

"But only look how well it has answered, Grace. The clever tale set about has largely been accepted. Caroline tells me there have even been sightings on the romance of Selina's elopement with her true love and Purford's noble action in releasing her."

An explosive snort from the end of the table caused her to add, "Yes, Justin, idiocy, but what would you? It serves our turn. And you will own, Grace, that your daughter has suffered no ill effects."

Jocasta jumped in, gurgling with delight. "The reverse, if anything. I have become quite the rage, Mama, you know I have."

The Dragon, not much to Marianne's surprise, was quick to take this up. "Lady Jocasta, that remark is quite unbecoming."

"But true," Justin cut in swiftly, casting his sister a quick smile.

"Yes, and I am ready to wager Aunt Pippa is right about you too, Justin. Any number of girls will be ready to have you throw the handkerchief."

"Well, as I am not about to throw any handkerchiefs, we shall never know."

"Of course he is not," snapped Grace. "No one could expect it of him. I wish you will hold your tongue, Jocasta."

Since she looked at Lady Luthrie as she spoke, Marianne guessed Grace was wishing to say as much to her sister-in-law. She had as well have spared herself.

"Ah, but that is precisely what concerns me."

This pronouncement was productive of a startled silence. Marianne felt as bemused as the rest. Nothing loth, Lady Luthrie pursued her advantage.

"I have been observing you closely, Purford, and it seems to me you are labouring under a good deal of strain."

Justin's lips tightened, but he did not speak. Marianne felt for him.

"You are in just that frame of mind," continued his aunt, "which is liable to send a young man off at half cock, which would be fatal."

"What do you mean, Philippa?" Grace was eyeing her stepson with bewilderment. "Justin has too much common sense to be taken in by any designing female."

"But has he enough to refrain from plunging into some ill-thought engagement?"

"On the rebound? Rest assured, Aunt, that I will do nothing so ill-judged. Good God, why do you think I've held aloof all these weeks?"

Marianne's jumping nerves steadied a little. She'd been so afraid he would succumb to one of the lures being held out to him.

"I am relieved to hear it," Lady Luthrie returned, in a measured tone. "That was not my fear, however."

"Oh? Then in what capacity do you think I am deficient, Aunt Pippa? Do you distrust my judgement?"

The note of sarcasm was not lost on Marianne, but it did not deter Lady Luthrie.

"The point, my dear boy, is that you have been so used to think only of Lady Selina, who was not of your choosing, it would be wonderful indeed if you had given thought to the type of female who will suit."

Jocasta, irrepressible as ever, broke in, eyes dancing. "Dear Aunt, surely that is a much better thing? Why, I have been told I don't know how many times how I should regard prospective suitors without prejudice."

"You are merely the daughter of an earl, Jocasta, though I am sure neither Grace nor Justin will countenance your union with any but a suitable parti."

"Like Selina, you mean." Justin's eyes were narrowed, a dangerous light warning Marianne at least that his temper was on a short rein. "No, Aunt. I shall not be constraining my sister's choice."

"Unless I choose some perfectly ineligible half-pay officer, or a fortune hunter. You said as much before I came out, Justin, you know you did."

"I have every confidence in your good sense, unlike our aunt has in me."

He turned his head as he spoke, his tone cool, and Marianne could only wonder at Lady Luthrie's apparent indifference.

"You need not poker up, Purford. Your father inculcated you with proper notions and I have no doubt you will make no misalliance. But certain considerations are unlikely to have occurred to you."

"Such as?"

Marianne felt as if the whole room held its breath, as she did. Nothing could be further from her wish than to hear a catalogue of the qualities Lady Luthrie believed must suit Justin.

"What you need after this debacle with Selina, though I dare say you don't think it, is a female with no missish scruples, who is not romantic and will therefore expect little or nothing from you in the way of attentions."

"How utterly soulless!"

"But sensible, Grace. Of course, she must be amiable and of good character and birth, but that goes without saying."

"What you are saying is that he must not fall in love," said Jocasta. "A bleak prospect for poor Justin."

Justin's lips were tightly compressed and Marianne's earlier suspicions revived. Of course he would not speak of it had he lost his heart.

"There is no reason why such a female should not feel affection for him, or he for her." Lady Luthrie's tones were as measured as ever, seemingly unmoved by the disapproval of all concerned. "My advice to you, Justin, is to look outside the crop of fresh debutantes. Find someone who has been out for two or three seasons, and is thus mature enough to be capable of fulfilling the arduous task of managing your household."

There was a short silence while several persons digested this. Grace looked disgruntled, Justin furious, the Dragon amazed, and Jocasta thoughtful. Marianne found she was still holding her breath and forced herself to let it go. And then disaster struck.

Jocasta suddenly raised her head, her eyes sparkling with mischief. "Aunt, do you realise you have exactly described Marianne?"

# Chapter Thirteen

A sensation of blankness overtook Justin, as if he had been hit in the head with a blunt instrument. His capacity to think deserted him and he was only conscious of Marianne's face, white and set.

She leapt from her seat and ran out of the room. Instinct took over and Justin was up and following before he could measure either reason or wisdom in the doing. Unthought words spilled from his mouth as he passed his sister's chair.

"You little idiot, Jocasta! How could you?"

Next moment he was in the hall, moving swiftly to intercept Marianne as she set a foot on the first stair.

"Wait!"

He grasped her arm and dragged her back. She turned ravaged features towards him, streaked with tears.

"Let me go, Justin! I can bear no more!"

He did not release her, rather tightening his grip. "I'm not letting you go in that state. Come into the morning room."

Without waiting for a response, he pulled her willy-nilly across the hall, flinging open the door to the morning room and pushing her inside. Only when he'd shut the door behind them did he allow her to pull her arm out of his hold.

She scuttled away from him and came up short against the fireplace, where she remained with her back to him.

Justin followed her, again pulling her about to face him. "Pay no heed to Jocasta's nonsense, Marianne. She doesn't know what she's talking about."

Her tears were arrested, but she was biting her lip. Jocasta's words hung in the air between them. Justin did what he might to deflect them.

"You've had a trying morning, my poor girl."

A faint grimace crossed her face. "You could say so."

"What happened with Grace?"

She shrugged and sighed. "Just what I might have expected."

"But you didn't expect it from her, did you? You were afraid of what the tabbies would say."

A hollow laugh escaped her. "I think she's turned into a tabby herself."

He was obliged to smile. "She's certainly behaving like one. What in the world made her so devilish cross? It's not as if you were flirting with every man in the place."

Her eyes reflected a trace of the distress he'd seen earlier.

"I don't honestly know, Justin. She was beside herself when she came into my chamber last night. She said I'd made a figure of myself, a fool of her." Her eye kindled. "And that I'd forgotten my place. That hurt the most, I think."

A burn of fury swept through Justin. "I should think it might! How dared she say such a thing?"

Marianne's lip quivered. "Well, in a way she's right. I am, if truth be told, but an adjunct to the family, with no real right to be in it."

"The truth, Marianne, is that you are the mainstay of the household. And Grace has selfishly allowed you to shoulder her responsibilities. Forgotten your place indeed! I've a good mind to give her a trimming."

Foreboding came into her face. "Pray don't! She's upset enough as it is."

"So are you upset and that is of far more importance."

Marianne's cheeks flew colour and she could not meet his eyes. Impelled, Justin grasped her hands.

"Don't let her browbeat you, my dearest girl. You are worth ten of Grace, you must know that."

She looked at him then, her eyes luminous, her mouth trembling. "I don't know it, Justin. But I'm grateful to my dear friend for saying as much."

The words were like a douche of cold water. Friend? He released her hands and took a step back, acutely conscious. Yes, that was how she saw him, had always done so.

Her brows drew together. "What have I said?"

He forced a smile. "Nothing. Oh, I was remembering my wretched aunt, I think."

The frown did not abate. "No, you weren't. You recoiled from me."

"I didn't recoil. Don't be ridiculous."

She eyed him in a way that made it hard to sustain his façade. But she did not pursue it, to his relief. "What do you mean to do?"

He was thrown for a moment. "About what?"

"Your future. I hate to own it, but there is much in what your aunt said. About me, I mean."

Now what was she at? "Why should it trouble you?"

"Well, you admitted that I have all but usurped Grace's position."

"I didn't say usurped."

"You know what I mean. If — no, when you marry, Justin, it's perfectly true that I cannot continue to do what I do."

"I don't see why not?"

"Don't you? Then you must be all about in your head!"

The asperity in her tone was so much more like her normal manner with him that Justin relaxed. "Marianne, it's not a matter of urgency, I assure you."

"It is for me."

The intensity of this remark shocked him. "Why do you say that? You never mentioned the matter when I was betrothed to Selina."

"Because I never thought about it."

"Until Aunt Pippa put it into your head."

She sighed. "Well, yes. She's right, much as I hate to admit it."

"She's an interfering busybody. She always has been. In fact, it's my belief it was her doing in the first place that —"

He broke off, aghast at what he'd been about to reveal. That was the trouble with talking to Marianne. So used was he to speak his mind without reserve, it was all too easy to trip. But then he'd never had to discuss this ticklish matter with the subject of it.

She was eyeing him with question in her face, though she refrained from asking. Was the trouble back in her eyes? He hastened to change tack.

"Never mind my aunt. She has the devil's own impertinence, trying to tell either of us how to run our lives."

A flicker of Marianne's characteristic tease showed in her eyes. "Well, if you will allow her to express her opinions without restraint, what do you expect?"

He had to laugh. "Yes, I ought to have squashed the woman at the first word. That's the trouble with females who have known you from the cradle. They can't easily be set down."

"Justin, you know perfectly well you are far too well brought up to be rude to your aunt."

A sliver of old resentment cut into him. "Yes, my father was thorough. He held himself on too high a form."

"Except when he fell in love with Grace and married her."

Justin was struck by the truth of this. He had never questioned his father's action in taking a second wife. And Grace was young enough and pretty enough to have been a dazzling stepmother to an impressionable youth. Before he'd come to recognise her die-away airs and tendency to make mountains out of molehills. He'd been too young at the time to see it, but that his father had married some distance beneath him had formed one of the arguments Justin used years ago when he'd done his utmost to justify the choice his father had forbidden him to contemplate.

"But you are my heir, my boy," had said Lord Purford, "and your mother was of excellent blood."

Justin had found it unanswerable. At the time. Later he'd felt it spurious, for what if he'd died? Any male offspring from the union with Grace must have taken his place. In the event, only Jocasta had survived infancy, so the question did not arise. But it could have. What price his father's placing himself on that high form then?

Marianne moved away from him and sank down onto the sofa, setting her elbows on her knees and dropping her face between her hands.

It was a pose he'd seen her adopt many a time: when she was deep in thought or wrestling with a knotty problem. He'd never before realised how touchingly vulnerable it made her, so used was he to her air of strong capability. She looked unusually youthful in the plain round gown of white muslin, modestly trimmed with cambric rather than lace.

"You've been under strain, too, haven't you?"

She looked up, and he could see it lurking at the back of her eyes.

"Damn Selina! She's plunged the lot of us into hell."

Marianne's hands dropped. He saw them clench, and her expression changed as she met his gaze with the bold courage he so much admired.

"Justin, I have a confession."

He braced. Now what? "Go on."

"I ought to have warned you. I debated within myself for days."

Bewilderment wreathed his brain. "What in the world are you talking about?"

"Lady Selina."

Foreboding gripped him. "Selina?"

Marianne's knuckles were white. "I saw her with that fellow. Gregory O'Donovan. In Hookham's."

Marianne had his full attention now.

"She — she presented him as an old friend. Before she noticed me, they were talking in a way that looked peculiarly intimate."

A rush of feeling enveloped him. The sense of betrayal revived, this time directed at Marianne. "Why didn't you tell me?"

She drew an obvious breath, but she held his gaze. "I could not make up my mind if I'd been mistaken. It was all suspicion and no real substance. If I was wrong, it would have cast a spoke in your wheel for nothing."

Hot words rose to his lips but he checked them. Marianne had not known how much he'd have given to be armed with such a spoke.

"I took care to watch their demeanour in public," she went on, "but I could see no hint of intimacy. Indeed, if I am to be wholly truthful with you, I was the more suspicious for the way they took care not to give attention to one another."

"Even though he formed one of her court," Justin returned, recalling an evening when he'd teased Marianne about the fellow.

"Yes. I never saw anything else, I promise you. I wish I had spoken. With hindsight and subsequent events, it seems criminal not to have done."

"That I cannot allow." His revived anger was dying. "Even had you spoken, on reflection I can't think it would have made any difference. Selina would have denied it. I believe she'd made her plans and meant to carry them out regardless."

"But she did mean to marry you before O'Donovan appeared on the scene, did she not?"

"It seemed so, but who can tell? She may have been waiting for him, for all I know. She refused to acknowledge the existence of a prior attachment."

"Yes, you said as much."

Marianne was fidgeting with her fingers still. Justin crossed to the sofa and dropped down before her, setting his hand on her restless ones and holding them fast.

"Don't refine too much upon it, Marianne. It's done."

"But it might have given you a chance to avoid the scandal had I said something."

"I hardly think so. Even if she'd admitted the thing and cried off our engagement, there would have been a deal of talk."

He rose, looking down at her bent head. They had strayed far from the point of his dragging her into the room. As well perhaps. At least the embarrassment of the moment had been glossed over.

He was distracted by the opening of the door. His sister's dark head peeped round.

"Have you settled everything? Can I come in?"

Marianne viewed the entrance of Jocasta with mixed feelings. She was calmer, but dead inside. The flicker of hope she'd cherished when Justin dragged her in here had been crushed. She did not know whether the interruption was a blessing or a curse.

"I don't know how you dare show your face," Justin chided.

Jocasta was not noticeably dashed. A giggle escaped her. "Oh, I know I should not have said it, my dearest brother, but it escaped before I could think."

"Yes, that's just your trouble, my girl. You never do think before you open your mouth. You embarrassed Marianne and you put me in an awkward situation."

Jocasta pouted. "I've already endured a scold, I thank you."

"You deserve one."

"Yes, but not three!"

"Three? Oh, you mean Grace and my aunt have already had their say."

"And the Dragon. But if you and Marianne insist on ringing another peal over me, I dare say I shall manage to endure it."

Amusement lightened Marianne's gloom. "Since no words of censure are likely to have the slightest effect, there seems little point."

Justin laughed. "Very true. You may consider yourself suitably chastised, Jocasta."

Uttering a delighted squeal, she flew to Justin and subjected him to a ruthless hug.

"Best of brothers!"

Extricating himself, Justin held her off. "That's all very well, but I'm not pleased with you, so don't think it."

Ignoring this, Jocasta came over to the sofa, flounced down beside Marianne, careless of crushing her muslin petticoats, and seized her hand, squeezing it tight.

"I should not have said it, I know, Marianne, but if you want the truth, I should like it of all things if you and Justin were to marry."

"Jocasta, for heaven's sake!"

Marianne felt her cheeks grow warm and was glad Justin's attention was on his sister.

"Well, why shouldn't I say it? I told you before I always thought the two of you would make a match of it, didn't I?"

Marianne saw Justin's jaw tighten and her heart sank. She could only be glad she had never given in to the temptation to touch on the matter herself. It was obvious the notion was anathema to him.

"Marianne, I can only apologise for my sister's lack of tact."

"Don't heed it," she managed, squeezing the hand still holding hers. With an effort, she summoned all her resources and smiled at Jocasta. "You are forgetting we are friends, my dear. Friends do not commonly marry each other. Besides, Justin has a duty to his name and I simply wouldn't do."

She glanced at Justin as she spoke and found him frowning. She could not read the expression in his eyes, but Jocasta did not wait for his response.

"Pooh, that's fustian! Justin, you can't be so stiff-rumped as to hold your nose up at Marianne."

"That will do!" Justin strode across to the door and opened it, looking back at his sister. "Out!"

The command was stern enough to cause Jocasta to release Marianne and eye him with uncertainty. Marianne would have preferred to leave herself, but she could not undermine Justin's authority.

"Jocasta, I mean it."

She looked from him to Marianne and back again. Her shoulders drooped. She got up and went to the door, where she paused, looking up at him. "I never thought you could be so horrid, Justin. After all Marianne has done for us all."

He flushed, but he did not speak, merely jerking his head to indicate she should go.

Jocasta left with a flounce and a toss of the head and Justin shut the door behind her with a decided snap. Then he turned to face Marianne and grimaced.

"Sisters!"

"Be glad you have only the one."

"She's as bad as my aunt, if you want the truth."

Marianne said nothing, consciousness returning in a bang. How in the world were they to get over this? Jocasta, in her innocence, had tipped them both into crisis. For her part, Marianne could not think their friendship would survive.

Justin crossed to the mantel and leaned his elbow on it, regarding the clock on the shelf with studied attention. Marianne doubted he saw it. The minutes lengthened. In vain she sought for something to say to ease the moment. Her mind refused to supply anything commonplace enough to serve. Instead it dwelled on the way his pantaloons outlined the muscled legs, on how the dark green coat set off his fair hair and the intricacy of his neck-cloth.

At last Justin's gaze rose from contemplation of the clock. Marianne met his gaze and the intensity there enhanced the green so strongly her breath caught.

"The devil of it is, Marianne, that she's right. I have been too stiff-rumped to take the plunge."

Marianne's heart began to thrum, threatening to rise up and choke her. She could not utter a word, all her faculties suspended.

The silence stretched until her nerves became unendurable and she had to speak.

"Justin, are you saying —?"

"That you should marry me, yes."

"Should?"

"No, I don't mean that. I mean, will you?"

"Why?"

She was riding on instinct. The words, so longed for, were not the right ones.

Justin shut his eyes tight, as if the sight of her could not be endured, and then opened them again. "Because — because Jocasta said what we all know to be true. You are the perfect chatelaine already. Purford Park depends on your offices. And we are friends. We have — affection — for one another."

"Affection, yes." This was worse than wanting it and knowing it could not be. "Is that enough, Justin?"

He uttered a mirthless laugh. "It's a deal more than I had with Selina."

Oh, this was unbearable. This was not how it should be. Not how she had imagined it. She'd feared his being snapped up by another and now she had her wish. He was actually offering for her. But for all the wrong reasons! How could she stop it?

"Justin, you must not let your aunt's jobations influence you. There is no need for such a sacrifice."

At that his eyes lit with wrath.

"Sacrifice? That's how you see it?"

"For you, I mean. You've no need to settle for me. You might have anyone."

"Supposing I don't want just anyone?"

Her heart thudded. Was he about to say what she yearned to hear?

He left the mantel and paced across the room and back again.

"Marianne, you know the circumstances. You are the last person to demand from me what it is not in my power to give."

Had she not known it? His affection had not the depth of hers. Did he imagine she could marry him and be content with that? She'd thought she could when she toyed with the notion of offering herself as substitute for Selina. But when it came to the point, could she bear to be intimate —?

The thought stopped dead. No! Impossible. To accept Justin's caresses, to endure the marriage bed, merely for the sake of his bloodline? Even as the prospect caused a rush of heat to flood her, she could not stop the refutation from leaving her lips.

"But you are asking more from me than I can give, Justin. It is not merely a matter of my continuing to fill Grace's shoes. You need an heir."

He was pacing again, but stopped in his tracks, staring at her, colour rising in his face.

"Is that … are you…?" He cleared his throat. "I would never force myself upon you, Marianne, surely you know that?"

Force himself! When all she'd ever dreamed of was to have his arms about her, his lips on hers? But in passion, not duty. Grace's voice sounded in her head. *How soulless.*

The words came fast and furious, though her tongue felt dry, stiff and unnatural.

"You are thinking of your aunt's speaking of a creature without missish scruples, but that isn't me. I have a fund of them, Justin. Every possible scruple you might care to name. I couldn't conduct myself like the conformable wife you are imagining."

"Conformable?"

He sounded both hurt and baffled, but Marianne's distress was too acute to spare him.

"Oh, one who will do as you require as and when you require it, make no demands for attention and keep her mouth shut at all other times."

"When have you ever done so? Why would I expect you to change?"

"But you would, Justin. You would expect it. Those — those marital duties aside, the things I say to you I can say because I am your friend, your confidante at times, though I know there are matters you will not speak of, even to me."

He threw up his hands. "Marianne, this is nonsense and you know it. How could a closer relationship drive a wedge through our friendship? The reverse rather."

"Yes, if we loved one another."

There. It was out. Now he would say they were bound to grow fonder if they were married, and break her heart at last.

Yet Justin said nothing of the kind. His jaw was set tight and he was eyeing her with an expression both frustrated and questioning.

"You don't wish to marry me, do you? This is mere quibbling, but you fear to hurt me with an outright rejection."

Heavens, what now was she to say? The dearest wish of her heart! But on these terms? Now her tongue clogged her mouth while her mind sought and cast out as worthless such words as came into it.

"Justin…"

He flung up a hand. "You need say no more. I see how it is. I was a fool to suggest it."

He was turning, clearly intending to leave the room. Marianne was up, moving swiftly to intercept him. She could not let him go like this. She grasped his arm and he halted. Dismayed, she searched his gaze. "I have hurt you! Oh, Justin, you don't understand."

"I understand only too well."

His features were rigid, the green dulled in his eyes. A shaft went through her. Fatal words hovered in her mouth. She had no chance to utter them.

With deliberation, he removed her fingers from his arm. His voice was ice.

"Don't fret, Marianne. Curse my aunt and sister instead."

The door shut behind him.

# Chapter Fourteen

Embarking on his third glass, Justin sagged back into the comfort of the club's padded leather chair and let his breath go in a long sigh. The brandy fumes wreathing his brain afforded, as he'd intended, a measure of relief from the raging thunder in his head. In minutes he discovered the indulgence had not clouded a corroding sense of disillusionment. He felt both a fraud and a fool, but his deepest dissatisfaction lay with the knowledge forced upon him that he had wilfully mistaken Marianne's sentiments.

Never once had it occurred to him, under all the agonies of indecision in which he'd laboured, both now and years ago, that he could meet with a rebuff. Had he misread her so badly? No, it was worse than that. Too wrapped up in his own feelings, he'd not taken time or effort to read her, to consider what might be her reaction. And thereby exposed himself to the most bitter humiliation.

Smarting and choked with conflicting emotions, he'd left the house within the minutes it took to reach his chamber and set the bell pealing for his valet to bring him his coat, hat and cane. He'd spent the intervening time striding restlessly about the room, his head full of fury and his heart heavy with loss.

The latter had not manifested as strongly as it did now, when the white heat of his first reaction had consumed him as he strode through the streets, determined only to gain the safety of Brooks's and commandeer a quiet spot where he might brood in peace.

Though Jocasta's unruly tongue had propelled him into that insane declaration, he was more inclined to blame his aunt. Without her prompting, his sister would not have said it.

He caught himself up on the thought. She had said it. Confronted with his betrothal to Selina, Jocasta had not scrupled to speak her mind. At the time, it had failed to pierce his armour. Months of steeling himself to the inevitable had eroded any vestige of regret lurking deep inside for what might have been. But within days of Selina's flight, it had sprung almost full-blown from the secret cache in which he'd long since buried it. He'd wrestled against the tug of need, beset by his father's voice in his head, drumming in the duty.

"Persons of our order, my dear Justin, do not marry to please themselves. There is too much at stake. By birth, you hold this heritage in trust for your heirs, and you owe it to them to maintain the purity of the bloodline."

He had protested, with all the vigour at his disposal, to no avail.

"You must not think I do not value Marianne, my boy. She is a good, sensible girl who has shown herself worthy of your stepmother's charity, but she will not do for you."

He balked at the remembered words, hearing instead Marianne's voice repeating the self-same litany. *She would not do for him.* Spurious, such words in her mouth. A convenient excuse, because she cared for him enough to wish to spare his feelings. Yet not enough to endure a more intimate relationship.

There lay the rub. Of all things, he could not shake the humiliation of discovering Marianne's aversion to physical closeness with him. It was of no use to tell himself it was because she thought of him as a brother. He had never felt that. She had been to him, almost from the first, all woman.

135

Only the impropriety of it had kept him from giving rein to his partiality. That, and his inability ever to predict Marianne's likely response, if he was honest.

From the moment he had found her in distress that far-off day, and teased her out of the dismals, she had laughed with him, teased him back, listened with unstinted interest and sympathy to such troubles as he entrusted to her ears, and proffered such advice as she might think of in her matter of fact fashion. But neither by word nor look had she ever invited his gallantry.

She'd accepted his touch without question, her hands ever ready to clasp his. Unlike Jocasta, who flew to his arms in childlike delight, Marianne had always kept a proper distance. Except when he tickled her.

There had been one or two occasions when her giggles, squeals and wriggling protests had brought him very near disgracing them both. But he could not recall Marianne succumbing to any such impulse. She invariably succeeded in throwing him off and escaping, several times becoming quite cross with him.

"Stop it now, Justin! That's enough! It's horrid of you to take advantage of my ticklish state."

In his arrogance, he had never supposed Marianne would not welcome his caresses. How should he think so when her eyes lit up at sight of him? When he had only to meet her gaze across a room to find warmth in her smile, affection in her manner? He had been grossly deceived!

The rush of resentment was swiftly succeeded by an equally fierce rush of guilt. He had deceived himself. It was clear enough now that Marianne's friendship had never included that tenderness he felt towards her. What had she said? *If we loved one another.* Which was as much as to say she did not love him. Or not in the way of marriage.

He could only thank his stars he had not put his heart on the line to be trampled as his pride had been. Let her think he had proposed the match as a matter of convenience. Better for him, and better for Marianne too.

Whatever her feelings, she could only be insulted by the truth. He had denied his own heart because he'd taken his father's dictum and deemed her unworthy. Never dreaming, of course, that she might refuse him.

"Starting early, ain't you, coz? What's to do?"

The well-known voice cut into his reverie. Justin looked up to find Lord Dymond standing over him, a disapproving frown on his face. Annoyance gripped him.

"What do you want, Alex? If my aunt has sent you after me, let me tell you —"

"Devil a bit, old fellow! Ain't seen the old lady this morning."

"Oh. Well, I wish I had not either."

"Bad as that? She been sticking her oar in again?"

The thought of his aunt sent Justin's hand reaching for the bottle, but his cousin grabbed it away.

"No, you don't, coz. Looks to me as if you've had more than enough already. Carry on like that and you'll be half-cut before dinner."

"Damn you, Alex, give that to me!"

But his cousin, sitting in the chair opposite, set the bottle down on a table beyond his reach. He then bent a glare upon Justin and wagged a finger.

"Not going to let you go down that road, my boy, so don't think it."

137

Justin hunched a shoulder. "What the deuce has it to do with you if I choose to go to perdition?"

"Of course it's to do with me. Fond of you, Justin. Besides, my cousin, you know. You'd do the same for me."

Undeniable. Justin fetched a heavy sigh and sank back again. Alex nodded, a grim smile creasing his mouth.

"That's better. Now cut line, dear boy. What's shoved you into the dismals? After last night, I thought you were set to brighten up."

"Don't talk to me about last night. I've heard enough of it to last me to the end of the season — if I don't turn tail and head back to the Park, as I can tell you I've a good mind to do."

"My mother been plaguing your life out?"

Recognising that his cousin would not leave it alone, Justin gave him a curt account of the morning's events, not omitting a bitter animadversion on his sister's idiotic behaviour.

"Always was a tactless little piece, Jocasta." Alex eyed him. "What did you say to Marianne?"

"All that was designed to gloss over the business." He hesitated, but the urge to unburden himself to the only man he trusted proved too strong. "And all that did just the opposite too."

His cousin's brows shot up. "Don't tell me you popped the question."

Justin winced. "She won't have me."

"She refused you?"

He shifted uncomfortably. "Not precisely. But she made it clear enough she didn't want — she'd no thought of —" He broke off, but Alex did not speak. As if impelled, he brought it out. "She made it plain she couldn't stomach me as a husband."

"I don't believe it! What, Marianne not wish to marry you? Girl's been head over ears for you for years!"

Justin stared at him in uncomprehending silence. Had his cousin made the same error he had? Alex might be pardoned for thinking what he had not hesitated to believe himself.

"You are mistaken, as was I."

"Balderdash!"

Justin sighed again. "I only wish it were, Alex."

"What exactly did she say?"

"I can't tell you." He was not going to repeat the substance of that humiliating conversation. "Besides, it makes no odds. I withdrew my offer."

"Well, all I can say is, old fellow, you must have made mincemeat of the business."

If only it were that simple. He'd made a fool of himself, he knew that much. But not even to his cousin's ears could he confide his true state of mind. Deep down, the erosion of all hope had begun, for he knew he'd lost the solace of Marianne's friendship as well as any chance of achieving his heart's desire.

Before what Marianne was fast coming to think of as The Day of Disaster, the Season had seemed interminable. Now its end hurtled towards her like a bolting horse. Bad as it was to be estranged from Justin in Town, she knew it must be a hundred times worse back at Purford Park. How much harder to avoid an accidental meeting there, when she must face him daily over the dinner table and could scarcely avoid contact when household matters demanded his attention.

That he had taken to dining at his club or with friends spoke volumes. When she entered the breakfast parlour, he had either ridden out or left for some unknown engagement. He cried off escorting his stepmother and sister to the last ball of the season, and only once did Marianne spot him at a perfectly insipid musical evening given by Mrs Guineaford.

She had not intended to go, but at the last moment Grace, as one might have expected, succumbed to her loathing of the hostess and developed a headache. Since Lord Tazewell, who was becoming very particular in his attentions, had offered to escort Jocasta, Marianne had no choice but to take Grace's place.

Her heart flipped when she saw Justin, in company with Alex and being besieged by a couple of determined matrons with marriageable daughters. Her breath caught in her throat and she lost the half of what Mrs Guineaford was saying to her.

"…and what is one to do when everyone is exhausted and itching to go home? So I hit upon this, my dear, where all that is required is to sit and listen."

"Most restful," Marianne managed, summoning a smile. She saw that more was required of her, and added, "The very thing, ma'am. A delightful notion. Lady Purford will be so disappointed to have missed it."

Mrs Guineaford smiled upon her with that complacent air Marianne knew infuriated Grace, and she was able to move on and catch up with Jocasta.

She knew without looking that Justin had seen her, for she could feel his inimical gaze. Her insides fluttered with an echo of the dreadful experience she had gone through after he left her on that appalling day.

She tried to push the memories aside, and succeeded to a degree while the company talked and partook of the delicacies on offer. Since she had not in public repeated the offence which had precipitated events, the censorious tabbies who had scolded her to Grace had condescended to forgive her. She was thus obliged to respond to enquiries about Grace's health while she kept a watchful eye upon Jocasta and tried, without success, to ignore Justin's presence.

Within moments of taking her place beside her charge, however, all attempts to keep out remembrance failed. To make it worse, Lord Tazewell had found seats at one side which gave her all too clear a view of Justin, who was sitting almost opposite, his long shapely legs disposed comfortably, with one ankle crossed over the other. He looked bored, though he kept his eyes on the harpist who had opened the proceedings. The bland expression beneath the fair locks transposed, in Marianne's mind, into the stiff effigy confronting her the last time he'd spoken to her in that alienating voice of ice cold rage.

She'd stood as if paralysed, unable to think or feel, until her legs had almost given way beneath her and she'd been obliged to sink into the nearest chair. She'd then been beset by hideous and unstoppable tremors that shook her frame from head to foot.

She hardly recalled those moments for both mind and feeling had frozen for the duration of what she afterwards recognised as the symptoms of shock. As well had she been told of Justin's death! The devastation to her heart was quite as bad.

No, not that. Marianne tugged her thoughts back to the present. Nothing could be as bad as that. Though she'd lost him as surely as if he had died. Curiously, she had not wept. Neither then, nor later in the privacy of her bed. She could only suppose herself too numbed to feel. Or perhaps the finality of her grief was too deep to be allowed to surface. She had found it surprisingly easy to assume a semblance of her normal manner. It was as if she dwelt in some other world, coiled there in a comforting ball, while her shadow walked and talked in this one, providing a substitute who could operate as needed.

It was well she had one, for she'd run the gamut of Grace's plaintive protests and Lady Luthrie's astringent ones.

"I have no wish to know what passed between you and Purford, my dear Marianne," said the latter upon encountering her a day or so after the debacle, "but it is plain enough that his conduct must have left a deal to be desired."

Under normal circumstances, Marianne would have rushed to Justin's defence. As it was, she remained tight-lipped, merely holding the woman's gaze. Lady Luthrie's brows rose.

"I see that you blame me for it. Well, perhaps I was unwise to interfere too directly."

"Or at all," returned Marianne, surprising herself.

The matron's faint smile acknowledged a hit, but she did not look conscious.

"Where one can see something needs to be done, it is cowardice to shirk the doing of it merely for fear of upset."

"A maxim you have lived by, ma'am?"

"Certainly. Is it not better to exert influence if one can than to bewail the consequences when one has done nothing to try to change them?"

"Like Grace, you mean."

Lady Luthrie gave a snort. "Grace has no moral fibre. I dare say my brother was to blame for that. He was besotted. He allowed her to indulge her megrims and did not check her tendency to fancy herself too frail to endure anything she did not wish to do."

Since Marianne knew this to be true, she made no attempt to refute it.

"We all have our faults, Lady Luthrie."

"And mine is to be an interfering busybody, is that it?"

Marianne had to smile, though she was far from laughter.

Lady Luthrie put out a hand and lightly touched her arm. "I am fond of you, Marianne. I wish I had known you better years ago. Still, I do not despair of a happy outcome."

With these words she had moved on, leaving Marianne mystified.

Grace, on the other hand, seemed heartily to dislike her. Her manner was cold and she openly taxed Marianne with having caused a rift within the family.

"You need not pretend that Justin's attitude to me is not your doing, Marianne. Heaven knows what you said to upset him so! But he was never discourteous to me before. You must have shown me in a bad light when you told him of our quarrel."

In vain did Marianne assure her they had not discussed it, but as she refused to divulge what had been said in the morning room, Grace obstinately insisted on believing she had been abused to her stepson, and complained of Marianne's heartlessness and ingratitude so frequently that it must have hurt her had she been less enwrapped in her protective shell.

Even Justin's absence in his studious avoidance of her had made no appreciable difference. Somewhere, her real self took note of it, adding to the store of hurts that miraculously passed her by.

But pinpricks of little agonies now plagued her, confronted as she was by Justin in person: the shift in his face when he had so completely misunderstood her hesitation. Her panic in that instant. And the stark recognition of her own wilful refusal to seize her chance.

She brushed the thoughts out of her mind. Concentrate instead on the music. A Haydn sonata? How dull it sounded. The harpist's execution was but competent, the piece interminable. She shifted her gaze to the Adam panels and the inset niches her hostess had caused to be bedecked with tall jardinières, flowers spraying from several orifices. It proved less distracting than the music.

A song followed, a duet in Italian performed in a reedy tenor by the man and an inadequate soprano by the woman. The disharmony scratched at Marianne's nerves until she wanted to shriek at them to stop.

The break afforded relief, but it quickly became apparent the stresses of the evening were not over.

"Give me leave, ma'am," said Lord Tazewell, with a slight bow towards Marianne.

He then walked quickly off, and Marianne turned to find Jocasta in a state of high excitement.

"He's going to ask Justin for an interview."

For a moment the implication passed Marianne by. "An interview?"

Jocasta changed her seat to the one next to Marianne and grabbed her hand, squeezing it painfully. She was clearly on the fidgets, but her cheeks were pink and her eyes sparkled. Marianne gazed at her in confusion.

"What in the world has put you to the blush, Jocasta?"

Her charge opened wide eyes. "Can you not guess, Marianne? And you so all alive!"

Realisation hit. "Has he offered?"

"No, but he is going to. When he saw Justin was here, he at once said he must speak to him. And he asked me if I should object. Of course I said no."

"But do you want to marry him?"

Jocasta puffed out a breath. "I think so. He is excessively amiable and he adores me."

The inevitable question sprang into Marianne's mind and she did not hesitate. "But do you adore him, Jocasta? Do you care for him at all?"

Jocasta looked flustered. "I don't know. I think I do. I like him very much at all events."

Instinct took over, despite Marianne's utter destruction of her own hopes and dreams. "Do not, I beg of you, Jocasta, marry a man you are not certain you love. Tazewell is no doubt eligible in every way."

"Well, he is," Jocasta insisted. "He's exactly the sort of man I am expected to marry."

"Yes, but —"

Her young cousin interrupted her without compunction. "I see what it is, Marianne. You won't enter the married state yourself, so you can't bear for me to do so either."

"Nothing of the kind! How can you think —?"

"Hush, he is coming back!"

Lord Tazewell was seen to be approaching, bearing a countenance that indicated his mission had prospered. Jocasta vacated his seat and he took it, leaning towards her, but Marianne overheard the whispered words.

"Tomorrow morning at ten o'clock."

A sick feeling entered Marianne's stomach. She acknowledged a sliver of truth in Jocasta's accusation. There would be celebrations tomorrow, a shower of congratulation that ought to have been hers.

An insidious thought stole into her mind. Had she agreed to marry Justin, would the news have been greeted with joy? Not by Grace certainly.

Marianne's heart began to hammer. Why had she not seen it before? Grace knew! She had long ago divined how Marianne felt. That was why she had told her about Lady Selina in the first place. Was that why she insisted upon an unmarried future where Marianne could only be her companion at the Dower House? She had been furious that night — was it not so much because Marianne had put herself forward, but rather because she had danced with Justin? If so, then she had wanted to know the substance of the fatal conference because she was afraid Marianne had succeeded. The reluctant conclusion must be that Grace was terrified of her cousin usurping her place.

Even in the hurt of such blatant self-interest, Marianne could appreciate these feelings. Grace had taken her penniless cousin into her home, out of kindness and charity. It was understandable that the thought of seeing the orphan elevated above her was anathema. And Grace was peculiarly jealous of her position at the best of times.

The cruelty of it cut at Marianne. Grace must be fully aware of how deeply Marianne loved Justin, yet she set the prospect of her own mortification above her cousin's happiness.

Well, she might rest on her laurels now, for the prospect no longer existed. And there was scant hope either Grace or Justin would put a bar in Jocasta's way.

The bleakness of her future stretched ahead of Marianne like a turbulent grey sea.

# Chapter Fifteen

Grappling with settlements and the contracts drawn up by the lawyers provided Justin with enough distraction at the start. Having been through this on his own account when he became betrothed to Selina, he found his attention focused on ensuring Jocasta's future security. Not that there was much difficulty. Tazewell was heir to a considerable patrimony and had taken possession of one of his father's estates upon attaining his majority. He'd been well taught and had a steady reputation. Jocasta had done very well for herself.

Tazewell was a few years older than his prospective bride, and was a model of sobriety, even in dress, favouring dark colours in coats that fitted without being moulded to his form and breeches covering his legs in preference to the more revealing pantaloons. Yet Justin had doubts of his ability to curb Jocasta's volatility. The man was clearly besotted, as his own father had been with Grace.

When the fellow had asked his permission to address Jocasta, Justin had found it hard to maintain his air of cool detachment. Under it, a streak of dismaying envy gnawed at him, forcing an obvious question. "Do you have reason to believe Jocasta returns your regard?"

Tazewell's pleasant countenance had reddened and he spluttered a little in his response. "Yes — yes, I believe I do, sir. She has not … well, I admit she has not said it in so many words. I mean, until I had spoken to you, naturally she would not be so forward."

Justin could not hold back a scornful laugh. "From what I know of my sister, Tazewell, a little matter of protocol would not deter her. Are you quite sure about this?"

The fellow's colour became more heightened still.

"Positive, my lord. I must marry, of course, but I had not hoped to find a female for whom I could feel that sort of … that sort of… In short, sir, I love her!"

This was flung at him with a defiance that could not but amuse Justin, despite its prick at his own deep disappointment.

"My dear Tazewell, pray don't imagine I disapprove. I am of your generation and I fully sympathise."

Looking relieved, Tazewell thanked him. "But do you give me leave to address Lady Jocasta?"

"I have no objection. Indeed, I cannot but be glad her choice falls upon a man as eligible as you, if you want the truth."

This had the effect of making the fellow flush again, and Justin felt compelled to enter a caveat. "The trouble is, Tazewell, I can't reconcile it with my conscience not to warn you that Jocasta is a flighty little piece with a mind of her own." He saw his words were making the other man's eyes kindle and threw up a hand. "Don't take me up wrongly. I'm as fond of my sister as I could be, and I've encouraged her liveliness. But she can be outspoken and pert."

Justin found himself under instant fire.

"Sir, your apprehensions are groundless. It is just these qualities that attracted me in the first place. Until I met Lady Jocasta, I had despaired of finding any but deadly dull, conformable creatures. But Jocasta is — is … well, she is very different, and if she will look upon my suit with favour, I assure you I will do everything in my power to make her happy."

After this, it did not surprise Justin to find his sister in raptures over the fellow. Whether her feelings went deep he could not judge, but he did not doubt her sincere attachment.

"Oh, how can you ask me, big brother? I have the greatest affection for my dearest Tom. He is the kindest creature and so attentive to my comfort. How could I not care for him?"

The flurry of excitement in the house served to lighten the dismal atmosphere that had prevailed since the hideous day etched in Justin's memory. But it afforded him little in the way of relief, since he was obliged to remain when Marianne was present. The sheer torture of being in the same room dulled after a while, but would not erase since she was as stiff as he knew himself to be. She might appear normal, but Justin knew her too well not to note the cracks in her armour.

Despite the hurt she had inflicted, he could not but be affected by a ripple at her cheek, a clench at her jaw or the trouble he detected behind her eyes. He was forced to conclude that the estrangement was almost as painful to her as it was to him, and his mood worsened.

Try as he might to deaden his feeling for her, he could not. It was rooted too deep. If only she'd cared as much. That she did care he could not conceal from himself. She was suffering, and he hated that. But a barrier had been passed and there was no way back that he could see. If he could recall his foolish offer, he would. Yet that would leave him just as he had been before, in an agony of indecision.

Well, he'd taken the plunge and where had it got him? To a dreadful place where Marianne was no longer even a part of his life, but an incubus in his heart that threatened a future as dismal as if he had married Selina.

In honour bound, he invited Tazewell to visit Purford Park, hoping it would serve the dual purpose of enabling the betrothed couple to become better acquainted and of distracting him.

Although Tazewell was largely in Jocasta's company, the necessity to entertain him cut into Justin's attention to a degree that began to irk him within a very short space of time. It was galling to have to watch the expansion of the couple's happiness in each other as he and Marianne became ever more distant.

In exasperation, Justin sent to his cousin and begged him to join them. A third gentleman added to the party would at least dissipate the close attention on Jocasta and her *dearest Tom*.

There should have been balm in the fact that Grace had begun to thaw a trifle towards her. To her consternation, Marianne could feel nothing but dismay and contempt.

She felt she received Grace's favour only because her cousin saw that the threat of a union between her and Justin was out of count. Perhaps too because her triumph in Jocasta's success had mellowed her dissatisfaction. And of course she wanted to crow.

Grace had basked for a mere week in the congratulation and envy of her acquaintance, and Marianne realised it was not enough.

"I always believed my lovely girl would do well, but as you know, my dear Marianne, I did not prophesy her making so brilliant a match."

"No indeed, cousin, you were more prone to prophesy disaster," Marianne returned before she could stop herself.

Grace flushed, but waved dismissive hands. "You mistake me. I did not wish her to acquire a reputation for impertinence."

"As well none of us succeeded in curbing her then, for Tazewell positively enjoys Jocasta's tactless outbursts."

"Nonsense, Marianne! How can you say so?"

"Because I know it to be true, ma'am. He confided to me that he believes they spring from naivety and a lively mind. He says he finds it both refreshing and endearing."

"It is odd in him, dear Lady Purford, but it cannot be regarded as other than a benefit." This from the Dragon, who was embracing with fervour her new role as Grace's official companion. "Such a well set-up young man, too. So truly the gentleman. His manner towards you, dear Lady Purford, I thought showed just the right sort of deference."

This flattery soothed Grace's ruffled feathers and she gave her attention with unconcealed preference to one who was more inclined to agree with her.

Marianne had been inordinately relieved when Justin, having settled the matter with Miss Stubbings, announced the arrangement at dinner a few days after the family's return to Purford Park. Her secret hope that it would release her from the burden of Grace's demands was dashed, for her cousin was too used to asking Marianne when she needed something done. Though these days, she did not trouble to couch her requests in the caressing way she had used in the past. Was she bent upon demonstrating Marianne's acceptable status?

In one thing, however, Marianne found herself redundant. She was no longer Grace's confidante. In her present dismal state, she was glad. But it hurt nevertheless.

Jocasta's shocked dismay at the Dragon's continued presence in the house amused Marianne, but she pointed out to the incensed damsel that she would not long be obliged to endure Miss Stubbing's company.

"Yes, and thank heavens for it! Well, Tazewell is anxious for an early date and I had demurred, since there is so much to do. But I declare I am so disgusted with Justin, I shall tell Tom I have changed my mind."

In the event, the endless discussions about the preparations for the wedding occupied all four ladies almost to the exclusion of anything else, until Marianne was ready to scream. If she could have absented herself from these sessions, she would have. But since she was the only one with any real competence in the matter of arranging such an event, she was unable so to do. Every question was referred to her as a matter of course, just as had been the case for the last several years. In turn, she consulted Mrs Woofferton, but in private so that irrelevancies were eliminated and they got on a good deal faster.

The arrival of Lord Tazewell put an end to this purgatory at least. Jocasta was rarely out of his company. Grace for once took up her position as lady of the house and played hostess, just as Justin was obliged to play host.

Marianne found herself able to reduce her public role. Behind the scenes, she continued to oversee all the domestic issues that a guest and his retinue of servants necessarily created as well as the normal operation of a large household and estate. Not that Marianne had anything to do with the tenancies or those tasks which came under Justin's jurisdiction as landlord. It was Marianne, however, who undertook the duties that lay more properly in Grace's orbit. She was glad of the excuse to absent herself with more frequency than she'd been able to do in the past.

There was old Mrs Soper to visit, and one of the women who had assisted with sewing the curtains for the new countess's apartments, who had fallen ill. A garrulous dame, Peggy did not allow Marianne to depart without a great many oblique questions about the end of Justin's betrothal. Since the matter was undoubtedly common knowledge all over the county, Marianne made no attempt at concealment, but steered the conversation into safer channels by dwelling on Jocasta's more promising upcoming nuptials.

She succeeded at last in bringing the visit to an end, and having made her farewells and left a basket of tasty provisions to tempt the woman's appetite, Marianne walked briskly back along the well-worn path through the trees edging the Park. It was a warm day, but a chill breeze made her glad of the short nankeen-coloured jacket despite the thick muslin petticoats of the plain round gown she'd donned for the expedition.

The path came out into the open grounds near the old oak with the integrated bench, and Marianne had the intention of stopping there for a breather.

As she came out of the trees, she saw the bench was already occupied. Her heart jerked, and thumped painfully as she took in the blond bent head, the dejected pose as Justin leaned his forearms on his thighs.

Just so had he sat that day — how long ago it seemed now — when she'd done her best to comfort him after Lady Selina's defection. His pain then echoed in her breast, and the realisation of his misery threw her back into the overriding guilt that had plagued her ever since The Day of Disaster.

She was tempted to sneak back into the trees and take the longer route around the lake via the little bridge that crossed it at the narrow end. Ridiculous. This was Justin, with whom she'd shared so much. Surely they could meet without falling out? So far, they had only been obliged to exchange the barest minimum of conversation, and that generally in company. Marianne had taken the precaution of ensuring Mrs Woofferton was with her when she was obliged to consult him about some domestic matter. Besides, she need only pass the time of day and move swiftly on.

The moment she shifted into the open, Justin turned his head and saw her. He sprang up from the bench as if scalded, and stood there, chin up and stiffening from head to foot.

Marianne's mouth was dry, but she forced herself to speak. "Don't disturb yourself. I am merely on my way back to the house."

Under the well-fitting blue frock-coat his shoulders relaxed slightly. "You've been on one of your missions?"

"Peggy Baker is ill. She helped with sewing the new curtains for the…"

Her voice died, the connotations of the preparations for Justin's abortive bride too near the bone for comfort. He did not take it up.

"I see." A faint smile showed for an instant. "You seized the chance to escape? I don't blame you."

An echo of the old familiarity spread warmth into the ice of Marianne's bosom. She gave a tiny laugh. "You too?"

He grimaced. "Tazewell is amiable enough, but…"

He stopped, the implication unspoken. Consciousness returned. Marianne could not doubt but that he was finding the bubbling happiness of the betrothed couple as trying as was she.

The little warmth dissipated and Marianne itched to be gone, even while the yearning to remain in Justin's company thrummed deep inside. But not like this when distance yawned between them.

"Well, I had best waste no more time."

He nodded and she turned to go. She had taken only a few steps when he spoke again. "Marianne…"

It was soft, almost too low to reach her. But it stopped her on the instant. She looked back.

Justin's features had softened and the expression in his eyes dragged at her wailing heart.

"Marianne, can we … is there no way back for us?"

The words cut at her misery. She took a few steps towards him.

"I wish there was, Justin."

He came closer until there was a bare couple of feet between them. "There ought to be a way. I miss my friend."

A lump formed in her throat and she blinked back the tears. "I too. Only…" She hesitated.

"Only?"

The prompt was accompanied by a swift frown, and the impulse to open her heart died. She adjusted what she had been going to say.

"Too much has changed."

"I have not changed!"

She felt it as an accusation. A spurt of anger seized her tongue before she could stop it. "Oh, so it is all my fault!"

"I didn't say that."

"You meant it. It was not I who brought the matter up, Justin."

"But you would not even pause to consider it."

"I did not need to. I already knew … I was well aware…"

His eyes blazed. "You need not say it again. I should have realised it, had I thought as I've since had time to think."

Confusion wreathed her mind. "What in the world does that mean?"

A muscle jerked in his cheek. "You've always held back, I see it now. The closer we became, the more you shrank from me."

"Shrank? What nonsense is this?"

"It's true, Marianne. You never would let me near you."

Shocked realisation stopped her tongue for a moment. He had wholly misread her. She had held off from him because she was afraid of giving herself away. But she could not say as much.

"If you mean I kept a proper distance —" He let out a snort of derision, provoking her into retort. "Besides, it's ridiculous to say so. Have you forgotten how I wept in your arms?"

"When you were a child!"

The scoffing tone threw her into irritation. "I was twelve and more, and all those years I never stood off from you."

"From the moment you grew into womanhood, Marianne, you would not let me touch you."

From which, it was evident from his tone, he inferred she found his touch unacceptable. Which was true, but not for the reason he thought. She had no defence, unless she revealed the truth, and that she could not do. She fell back upon a manner as derisive as his own. "It is absurd to bring up my conduct then. We are both of an age to be able to make a decision based upon present circumstances."

"Oh, you made your decision very clear. I could be in no doubt of your sentiments."

Marianne tried to hold back, but the revived hurt was too acute. "You never asked me what my sentiments were, Justin. You threw your offer at me without the slightest preparation. If it could be called an offer!"

"Because I was unprepared. It happened too fast. I had not considered…"

"No, you had not considered what it must mean, how it would affect us both. And you had no doubt of my accepting you."

She saw the truth of that in his flinch. But his eyes glittered.

"Well for me that you did not. You need not fret. I have no intention of repeating the offence."

She watched him stride away, all annoyance dissipating as despair gripped her. A way back? Dear Heaven, there was an ocean between them!

A yearning to be rid of the whole affair rose up. She ought to leave Purford Park. If she had means to do so, she would. She might look for a post. As companion or housekeeper, for either of which she was well qualified. Though whether Grace would provide her with a reference was another matter. Unlikely, since she would much dislike to be thought ungenerous enough to send her cousin out in a menial capacity.

No, there was only one means of escape. Perhaps Lady Luthrie was right. A marriage — any marriage as long as it was not with the man she loved — would secure her future and take her away from this well of despond.

# Chapter Sixteen

With a sigh of satisfaction, Justin watched his cousin sink into the chair opposite, the looser buff breeches and dark purple frockcoat for country wear permitting him to stretch his long legs as he made himself comfortable, crossing his feet at the ankles.

He had not realised how much he liked and relied upon Lord Dymond. Their friendship had been formed in childhood and at school, where they had rallied in support of each other against rival gangs of boys. As adults, they frequented the same clubs and moved in the same circles. Justin trusted him as he knew he was trusted in return, and next to Marianne, Alex had ever been his adviser and confidant.

Had been. Relations with Marianne being all but severed, his cousin necessarily moved into the role of adviser-in-chief.

Alex took a sip of the Madeira thoughtfully provided by his host and grinned across at him. "Had enough of your sister and her betrothed smelling of April and May?"

Justin let out a groan. "You may say so with confidence. Tazewell is well enough. In fact I like him, but it's the devil's own work to entertain the fellow when all he wants is to make sheep's eyes at Jocasta."

A bark of laughter escaped his cousin. "Should think you must be wishing the pair of them at the devil. That why you wanted me?"

Justin smiled. "A little leaven, Alex. And I hoped you might help me keep the fellow occupied while I attend to business. Higman is champing at the bit."

"Your agent, eh? Well, what do you need me for? Leave the fellow to Jocasta. Seems keen enough to spend all day with her."

"Of course they can't be allowed to roam at large without let or hindrance, you nodcock. Grace would have my head if I permitted it."

"True. Don't want to be obliged to hustle the wench into church."

Justin shuddered. "Don't raise spectres, Alex. We've had quite enough scandal this season, I thank you."

His cousin gave him a sympathetic look and sipped at his wine. But Justin began to feel uncomfortable as he noticed Alex was regarding him over the top of his glass. He knew that look.

In a bid to deflect question, he tossed off the remaining liquid and rose to pick up the decanter, holding it over his cousin's glass. "A top-up, coz?"

"Just a smidgeon. Don't want to appear top-heavy before the ladies."

For a few minutes, they sipped in companionable silence and Justin hoped he had laid his cousin's suspicions to rest. In vain.

"What's to do, old fellow? You didn't summon me here merely to play gooseberry between Tazewell and your sister."

Justin grimaced. "It wasn't a summons."

Alex's brows shot up. "Hoped I might enjoy a couple of day's shooting? Know you better than that, old fellow."

Which was all too true. Justin had held out the lure of taking out a gun in hopes of disguising his real need. He should have guessed Alex would see through it.

"You always were astute. You must take after Aunt Pippa."

Alex disregarded this. "Still blue-devilled?"

Justin capitulated. "If you must have it, I think I am going mad! I can't concentrate, my sleep is all to pieces and if you ask me what I ate this morning, I couldn't tell you. And it's of no use to say I should make it up with Marianne because I've tried and it's hopeless."

Alex surveyed him without speaking for a few minutes. Justin shifted under that penetrating scrutiny, but the relief of speaking out at last was greater than his embarrassment.

"Want me to intercede for you?"

Startled, Justin blinked at his cousin. "No! No, if anything is to be said it must be between Marianne and myself."

"Then tell her how you feel, man!"

The instant recoil inside made Justin throw up a hand. "And open myself to more of the same? No, I thank you."

Alex sat up, leaning his arms across his knees and nursing his glass between his hands. "Then answer me this, Justin. Given that Marianne doesn't care for you as you do for her — not that I believe it for a moment — would you still wish to be married to her, knowing that?"

Arrested, Justin stared at him. It was a new notion, and distinctly unpalatable. All these weeks, he'd laboured under the conviction that he wanted Marianne — at any price.

Jocasta had spurred him into action, breaking through his dilemma, weighing his desire against his late father's express prohibition. He'd spoken, put his fate to the touch, and Marianne had withered him in seconds.

Not for an instant had it then occurred to him she might not wish for a closer relationship, the intimacy he craved. He'd been smarting ever since, blaming her for what she could not help.

Did he want her on such terms? Could he be content, faced with a wife who had as little desire for his caresses as had

Selina? Could he take her, knowing she did not want him? Knowing she was reluctant? Repulsed perhaps?

Even as the question entered his mind, he knew it to be impossible. Was that why he'd been so furious with her? Because he knew, deep down, he could not endure to marry her under these circumstances?

He came out of his unpleasant reverie to find Alex still watching him. He hoped his thoughts had not been mirrored in his face, and felt heat rush up as consciousness claimed him.

"Well, coz?"

Justin drew a breath and let it slowly out. "No, Alex. You're right. I couldn't endure it." He became aware of a gleam of amusement in his cousin's eyes and balked. "I am glad to afford you entertainment."

To his chagrin, Alex laughed out. "Devil a bit, old fellow. Ain't at your expense. At least, it is, but not in the way you think."

Acid entered Justin's voice. "Then I will be obliged if you will explain yourself."

Alex lifted his glass to his lips and drained the remaining Madeira. Then he set the glass down on a convenient table at his elbow and fixed his cousin with a stony stare.

"Time you stopped thinking only of yourself, Justin." His cousin gave him no chance to refute this charge, holding up a hand even as he opened his mouth. "Know what you're going to say, but look at it."

"Look at what?"

"Just going to tell you, old fellow. No need to snap my nose off."

Justin begged his pardon, aware he sounded frigid. "Well?"

"Take the matter in reverse, my dear coz. Do you think Marianne would wish to be wedded to you if she knew she cared for you more than you do for her?"

The thought was blinding in its novelty. Justin could only gaze at his cousin, the notion revolving in his head, knocking his convictions apart. Was it possible? But she had recoiled from him. She'd made it all too clear she dreaded the intimate side of marriage. She'd been the one to raise the issue of his needing an heir. If we loved one another, she'd said. That could only mean one thing. Or could it?

"Alex, you have set my head in a whirl. Would you have me put it to the test?"

"How else do you expect to find it out?"

"I don't know." Justin set down his glass and thrust frustrated fingers into his hair. "No other way, I must suppose. Unless… Would you —? No, I couldn't abide that either."

"Then there's no hope for you, old fellow. Best make up your mind to marry someone else."

Marianne found it pleasant to walk with someone who did not have any axe to grind with her. The suggestion to get out into the fresh air had come from Alex and she was glad enough to agree. They ambled in the direction of the lake and watched the ducks and swans diving for their food. The innocuous topics entered upon in a desultory fashion soothed Marianne.

Had Lady Luthrie embarked upon her summer visit to her married daughter? She had, but it was married daughters in the plural now, Alex reminded her, since Georgiana, a deal harder to please than her cousin Jocasta, had at last been shuffled off in the previous autumn. However, his mother intended a longer stay with Charlotte, who was increasing again. And Alex was only too glad to take a bolt to Purford Park, since his father had taken it into his head to instruct him in the intricacies of estate management.

"Seems to have some notion he'll pop off without warning. Balderdash, of course. Sound as a roast, my father."

"But you must needs learn the ropes surely, Alex?"

"Good God, as if Outram ain't dragged me in any time these six years."

"Lord Luthrie's steward?"

"Says my father won't think of it if he don't, and he'd as lief I knew what I was doing before the need arises."

"He sounds a most forward thinking man."

"Fellow's a worse tartar than my mother, if you want the truth. Scares me to death."

Marianne laughed. "You'll have to assert your authority, Alex."

"Pooh! — to quote my cousin Jocasta. He'd see me off in a winking. Not like Justin's fellow Higman, who's bleating because he ain't been paying enough attention to his affairs. Outram would have his nose to the grindstone and no questions asked."

"Ah, but Higman is only Justin's agent. I imagine your father's steward is much more integrated into the household. You must have noticed how servants of long standing are inclined to become dictatorial."

"Like that Dragon of Jocasta's, you mean? What the deuce possessed Justin to foist her onto your cousin Grace? Should have pensioned her off."

"Yes, that is what Jocasta thinks." She hesitated, but felt Alex was trustworthy enough to be consulted. "To tell you the truth, I've wondered that myself, though I was glad of it."

"Should think you would be. Must be the very devil pandering to Grace's —" He broke off, reddening. "Beg pardon, Marianne. Shouldn't speak so of your cousin."

She returned a faint smile, misliking the reminder of the shambles in her domestic life. "It makes no matter. Grace can be trying, it's true."

From the way he kept his lips tightly closed while his eyes smouldered a little, Marianne guessed he felt this to be an understatement. Which indeed it was. She sought for mitigation.

"Well, it has freed me enough that I can think of taking Lady Luthrie's advice."

"Ah. Been plaguing your life out, has she? Know she took it into her head you ought to get riveted."

Marianne began to walk again, impatient of the subject and not wishing to have to look at Alex as she spoke of it. Without intent, she took the route that led the long way around the lake.

"It was good advice, as I've begun to perceive. I can scarcely remain here, and although I thought I might look for a suitable post, I cannot think Grace would promote such a thing."

"Nor Justin neither. Good God, Marianne, have you run mad?"

She glanced at him, unable to help a riffle of amusement at his shocked expression. "I don't think so, Alex."

"Then what should take you to fashion such a hare-brained scheme?"

"I haven't done so. Did I not say I knew it would meet with disapproval?"

"And well deserved!"

"No, why? When all is said and done, what have I been in this house but a companion and something of a housekeeper?"

Alex halted in his tracks, positively glaring at her. "Never heard such fustian in my life! Not such a nodcock as not to see you're a deal more than that. And don't try your flummery on me, Marianne. House wouldn't run without you. Justin's said so to me a score of times."

Smiling, Marianne tucked a hand into his arm and urged him onward. "Very well, I concede there is some truth in that. But as I told you, I have rather hit upon marriage as a more acceptable solution."

"Marriage to whom, may I ask?"

The heavy sarcasm in Alex's voice was not lost on Marianne, but she chose to ignore it. "That I have not yet discovered. I could advertise, I suppose."

"Advertise? You're bamming!"

"I'm not. You may often see advertisements of the kind. I am led to believe there are plenty of gentlemen willing enough to take a female without means, who will instead supply them with an excellent housekeeper."

Alex exploded with laughter. "Now I know you're roasting me. Housekeeper be damned, saving your presence! Wish you would cease teasing and pay attention."

Marianne's laugh sounded hollow to her own ears, but since she had no real intention of carrying out such a crazy plan, she allowed him to call a halt. "To be truthful with you, Alex, I have not yet fathomed how I should find someone suitable. Perhaps I will beg your mother for her help. She offered as much, after all."

"Don't need to do anything of that nature," stated Alex severely. "I'll tell you just what to do. If you're set on a marriage of convenience, you'd much better take Justin."

165

Her insides clenched and she pulled her arm out of his in a bang. "That would be far from convenient. Besides, he has withdrawn his offer."

"Makes no odds. He's still desirous of marrying you."

Marianne stopped dead, turning to confront him. "Alex, I wish you will not persist in this subject. Why do you imagine I'm looking to marry elsewhere? All is at an end for me in Purford Park, you must see that."

"I don't. All I see is you and Justin behaving like a couple of mules. And for what? Good God, anyone with eyes can see it's been a case between you for years!"

"You are mistaken."

Her voice tight, her heart leaden, Marianne turned to walk again, this time as briskly as she could. She almost ran towards the bridge, as if she must get away from a discussion as hurtful as it was hateful.

"Hey, wait!"

Alex caught up with her as she stepped onto the stone bridge with its balustrades fashioned from curlicues of iron. Marianne paused in the middle, grasping the railing and staring into the shallow waters below.

The silence became so fraught with unspoken dialogue that she let out a sound between a groan and a scream.

"Feeling better?"

She found herself laughing and became aware of tears trickling down her cheeks. She lifted a hand to dash them away, making a move towards the other side. Alex put out his hand to detain her.

"Not like you to turn into a watering pot. Here!"

Marianne found a handkerchief in front of her face. She grabbed it with a furious gesture and scrubbed at her eyes and cheeks. "I'm not crying!"

"Ah. Wind got in your eye?"

She was obliged to smile, and emerged from the handkerchief to find Alex grinning down at her.

"Know what, Marianne? I'm half minded to offer for you myself."

An outraged laugh escaped her. "For the Lord's sake, Alex! That would assuredly put the cat among the pigeons."

"Can you imagine Justin's face? Almost worth it just to see that."

"I wish you will stop being nonsensical. Not that I'm not grateful to you, but really, that is the outside of enough."

"Is it? Worse than marrying Justin?"

"Oh, stop! There is no comparison. I like you very well, but I would not dream of inflicting myself on you. And if you wish to think of faces, imagine your mother's!"

His eyes positively popped with shock. "Hadn't thought of that. She'd kick up the devil of a dust."

"She and Grace both. It's bad enough with Grace virtually disowning me for daring to think of marrying Justin."

"She wouldn't like it? I'd have thought it would suit her to a cow's thumb."

Marianne sighed as she turned to leave the bridge. "Oh, Alex, you don't know her at all, if that is what you think. I can't precisely blame her, for I can see how galling it would be to have her charity thrown back at her."

"How so?"

"By seeing me elevated above her, of course."

"Well, if that's so, seems shockingly selfish to me."

Marianne refrained from pointing out that Grace's self-absorption was one of the crosses she had to bear, and was responsible for her taking so much control in the household.

No more was said for a while as they followed the path through a batch of trees and came out at last upon the rough area of greensward, where the oak bench could be seen at the edge of the park.

The walk had tired her more than she knew, and Marianne suggested they should take a rest on the bench. She regretted it almost at once, for the memories crowded insistently into her head, culminating in that last quarrel with Justin. On impulse, she turned to Alex.

"It is over, Alex. There is no hope. If you want to find a way to help me, as I see that you do, it would be a kindness to cease to torture me by referring to this subject."

Alex sat half-turned towards her on the seat a little to one side, and his frown gave him a gloomy aspect. "Yes, but seems to me there's a deal more to it, Marianne."

"What do you mean?"

"Why should it be torture to you? If you don't care for Justin —"

She could not let this pass. "When did I ever say I did not care for him?"

"Well, I'm damned if I see why you'd refuse him if you do."

She tried to damp down the rise of distress, tightening against the hollow within her chest, swallowing the lump in her throat and blinking back the wetness at her eyes. But she could do nothing about the huskiness in her voice. "Oh, why can't you see, Alex? Why can't anyone see? It's not that I don't care enough. I care altogether too much!"

Remorseless, as it seemed to her, Alex pressed for more.

"You love him? You admit that?"

"Of course I love him. I've loved him from the first. But…"

She sighed, unable and unwilling to say it aloud. The words were taken out of her mouth.

"But you think he don't love you."

She could barely get it out. "Not in … not in that way. Oh, I know he does not. He would have — a long time ago, I thought — but it wasn't so. I've known for years."

In a deep corner of her mind, she'd hoped for refutation. But in the saner part, she knew it could not come. How should Alex know his cousin's mind? He'd mistaken their affection as friends for something warmer. After all, he hadn't known how deep her feelings ran. How should he? It was inconceivable that Justin would confide as much, even to his trusted cousin.

Her cheeks were wet again, and she discovered Alex's handkerchief once more being proffered. She could not remember giving it back to him.

She held it to her eyes, trying to pull herself together and control the flow.

A strong arm came about her. "That's it. Have a good cry. Make you feel better."

A watery chuckle escaped her, so incongruous was it to hear such words from Alex. Almost without conscious thought, she sank against him and laid her head on his willing shoulder.

It was comforting to lay her burdens down, even for this little time. Her tears ceased, but she remained where she was, her eyes closed, as a measure of peace seeped into her bosom. The sun was as warm as Alex's supporting arm and that portion of his chest upon which she lay, and she sighed with relief.

Marianne had no idea how long they remained thus, but it could not have been many minutes when Alex abruptly stiffened and an icy voice spoke.

"I trust you will forgive my intrusion."

Marianne sat bolt upright, heat flying into her cheeks. Nothing could have prevented her from shifting a little away from Alex on the bench, and she was immediately furious with herself for doing so. It made the situation look a deal worse than it was.

Alex leapt to his feet, his voice rough with scorn. "You don't intrude, coz, as you'd know perfectly well if you'd a grain of sense in your head."

Justin's gaze swept over his cousin and landed on Marianne. She felt scorched by the fury there.

"Oh, I've sense enough to believe the evidence of my own eyes." He turned back to his cousin. "I suppose you will pretend you were administering comfort?"

"No pretence about it. Exactly what I was doing."

The snap in Alex's voice alarmed Marianne more than Justin's anger. She pushed herself to her feet.

"Stop this, if you please. Both of you, stop it now."

Alex's glare moved to her face. "Won't have him casting aspersions, Marianne, so don't think it."

"And I will not allow this nonsense to come between you. Are things not bad enough as it is?"

"Whose fault is that?" Justin threw at her.

"That'll do, coz!"

Justin dropped a step back in face of his cousin's threatening stance. He made an obvious effort to rein in his temper. "I came to tell you both there is an expedition planned and Jocasta insists upon your presence." He waved at the bench, his tone taking on sarcasm. "But don't let me interrupt whatever it was you were doing."

"Any more, coz, and I'll plant you a facer!"

"You may try!"

As the two men squared up to one another, Marianne cut in, furious. "Will the two of you stop behaving like schoolboys? There was no impropriety here, Justin, and no reason for you to carry on like a bear with a sore head. You ought to be ashamed, accusing Alex. He's too much your friend to serve you a backhanded turn. Besides which, I am not yet your property!"

Her own words echoed in her head and she stood aghast. Justin's countenance changed as he took in the implication, and question entered his eyes.

Alex's raised brows told her he had made the same leap.

Appalled at her slip, and too distraught to think how in the world to retrieve it, Marianne fled the scene.

# Chapter Seventeen

Jocasta had rounded up the entire party, herding everyone into carriages, and declaring it was too hot when Justin and Alexander proposed riding beside the landaulet.

"In any event, it will not do for the two of you to be smelling of horses."

"Why, when you only propose to visit Zouch's Monument?"

Jocasta waved agitated hands in her brother's face. "We are meeting Mrs Ibbotson there, did I not say?"

"Who the devil is Mrs Ibbotson?"

"Good gracious, Justin, have you not been listening to anything Tom has told us? Mrs Ibbotson is his sister!"

Fortunately, Lord Tazewell was not in the parlour at that moment where the family had been requested to foregather.

"Indeed, we all remember that," Marianne cut in smoothly. Though why she should be flying to Justin's rescue, she really did not know. "But did not Lord Tazewell mention she lived nearer to his parents?"

"Oh, she has not come from Warwickshire. She sent to Tom this morning to tell him she was staying with her husband's grandmamma, and she is only at Send Place — and Send is scarcely six miles from here."

At this point, Lord Tazewell entered the room, just as Justin was demanding to know why they should all be dragged off to Zouch's monument when Jocasta might very well go and visit Mrs Ibbotson at Send Place.

Tazewell coloured a trifle, causing Jocasta to cast her brother a darkling look. Lord Dymond, to Marianne's relief, saved the day.

"Well, I'm game. Haven't seen that old monstrosity for years."

But it was evident Jocasta's betrothed felt an explanation was called for.

"You see, Purford, my sister declares these obligatory visits are nothing short of purgatory. She says the children are fractious and she must escape the Place. I knew she would be visiting soon, but had no notion she was already there."

Justin visibly dragged his irritation under control. "Must it be today?"

"Yes, for there is no saying when she may find another opportunity. It seems the old lady is keeping her bed, so Harriet begged me to bring Jocasta to meet her."

"She cannot wish to have the lot of us descending upon her. Take Jocasta. And Grace may play propriety."

Tazewell began to look harassed and Jocasta took a hand.

"Oh, Justin, do stop making foolish objections. Tom wishes you all to become acquainted with Mrs Ibbotson, for she rarely comes to Town."

"You may otherwise never meet her, for it is useless to go to the Place," added her betrothed. "By all accounts Ibbotson's grandmother is too frail and cantankerous to tolerate visitors. I thought it an ideal opportunity."

After this, there could be no further argument. Grace entering the room a moment later, agog and eager for the treat, neat in her muslins with a short cloak of yellow taffeta trimmed with black lace thrown over, the whole party set forward in short order. It had not been thought necessary to change out of casual morning dress and as the day was particularly fine, Jocasta contented herself with a tippet of white cambric muslin, while Marianne donned a short hussar jacket made of nankeen. All three women, however, were careful to wear straw bonnets against the glare of the sun and the men wore hats, but did not trouble themselves with great-coats over their frocks.

Marianne occupied the forward seat in the landaulet, alongside Grace, facing Jocasta and Tazewell. She was thus unable to avoid the sight of the phaeton which Justin was driving behind them, accompanied by Alex.

It was hard indeed to maintain a spurious pose of fluttering interest when Marianne's attention kept straying to the other carriage. Had the cousins made up their differences over Justin discovering Marianne in Alex's embrace? They looked to be chatting easily, but that might be a pose. The thought of what might have been said kept her nerves at stretch.

Had Alex betrayed her confidence? She knew him to be close with his cousin. He'd made his sentiments clear. She was inclined to think he had been on a mission when he invited her out to walk. Had Justin's hand been behind that? No, for he would not then have fallen into foolish error. Unless — could he have asked his cousin to discover her state of mind? Or was it Alex's notion to tackle her on the subject?

That he'd done so with intent she no longer doubted. And she had revealed what was in her heart.

Had they discussed her at all? They had not been more than a few minutes behind her. Long enough to have exchanged words that at least enabled them to give an appearance of harmony. Justin was obviously still out of temper, but she could not judge of Alex. Nothing could be settled now in any event, for the presence of Justin's groom up behind would prevent private discussion.

She was relieved that Grace's eager questions allowed her to take little part in the conversation in the landaulet. How long had Mrs Ibbotson been married? And how many children had she? Three already? And only four and twenty! What were their ages? She could not wait to meet the little dears, for she doted on infants. And a great deal more in this strain.

Marianne did not know whether to be glad or sorry the Dragon had been excluded, for Tazewell was looking battered by this catechism. Miss Stubbings might have curbed it, or even added to it, although she was more likely to have been obliged to ride on the box seat with the coachman. Which might be why Miss Stubbings had pleaded a headache, but Marianne suspected she had absented herself because she knew Jocasta would not welcome her presence. Marianne could wish she was herself on the box seat, since she would at least have been spared the ordeal of watching Justin.

At any other time, a drive in such sunny weather would have been pleasant, and the distance not too great to engender tedium. The Monument became visible well before they reached the lane that led to it. The carriage rolled past but from her position, Marianne could still see the edifice and was able to keep her eyes on the domed roof of the folly that was Zouch's Monument, below which were the familiar small pillars under arches set all around the slim tower, which at least enabled her to focus her attention on something other than Justin.

A couple of hundred yards down the lane, the landaulet rolled to a halt and the phaeton slid into place next to it. The grooms jumped down and went to the horse's heads, and Tazewell got down so that he might help the ladies to alight.

As Marianne stood up to leave the carriage, it became evident Mrs Ibbotson had arrived before them. A large coach stood near the trees. The horses had been removed from the traces and were grazing nearby. A set of rugs set with cushions had been placed under the trees and a lady armed with a parasol was seated there.

Marianne's gaze took in several small children playing close to the base of the tower, which looked a good deal wider and higher now they were closer, in company with a gentleman and a female Marianne took to be a nurse. Lord Tazewell, giving Grace his arm, and with Jocasta at his side, led both towards the lady under the trees. The latter sprang up and came to meet them. Justin and Alex had by this time alighted from the phaeton, and Marianne made haste to follow the others in order to avoid having to talk to them. The children were being ushered towards the party under the trees and in a very few moments, the hubbub of greetings took precedence over everything else.

Harriet Ibbotson was a comely young woman, who resembled her brother in looks but not character. She had the same brown eyes, curling dusky hair worn under a chip straw hat tied under the chin in a jaunty bow, and her plump cheeks mirrored a buxom form clad in a gown of sprigged muslin with a handkerchief tied about the neck and bosom in the old-fashioned way. Her attention was scattered; she bubbled from one subject to another without effort and was at once in raptures over the engagement and Jocasta herself.

"I declare, I had despaired of Tom coming to the point with anyone, but I am heartily glad of it now. Mama will be delighted with you, I know it. High time, Tom! But I will not tease you, for I cannot think of a better choice."

She carried on in this manner for several moments, until checked by her husband, a quiet man some years older than his wife, whose plain frock coat and buff breeches, comfortably loose, proclaimed the country squire.

"How you do run on, Harriet, my dear. You must allow poor Lady Purford to edge in a word."

Grace at once disclaimed, fearing Mrs Ibbotson might be crushed, but not a bit of it. She laughed heartily.

"Oh dear, am I doing it again? My tongue runs away with me. Dear Jocasta — may I call you Jocasta? — come and sit by me, do. And Lady Purford too, of course. Then we may enjoy a comfortable coze while the others enjoy the view."

With which, she waved dismissal at the remainder of the party and fluttered down upon the cushions, fussing as she made Grace and Jocasta comfortable. Marianne saw that Mr Ibbotson and Tazewell began to make conversation with the other two gentlemen, and slipped quietly away on the pretext of watching the children at play.

To lend credence to this, she spent some time attempting to draw out a shy little girl, younger than her two boisterous brothers, but brave enough to wish to emulate their prowess in running around the Monument as many times as they could without getting out of breath. Little Miss Ibbotson inevitably came to grief, and Marianne joined the tutting nurse and bent down to discover what injury had been sustained.

Discovering a strange lady beside her was enough to arrest the child's tears, and she stared at Marianne with a finger in her mouth and one hand clutching her nurse's skirts.

"What is your name?"

"Answer the lady, Miss Elizabeth."

"Oh, are you Elizabeth? Do they call you Lizzy?"

The child nodded and removed the finger from her mouth, displaying a lisp as she answered. "Lithybet."

"She can't say it yet, ma'am."

Marianne smiled at the child. "Well, there is time enough to learn to say it right."

She remained talking to the girl for a while, although she could not be said to have got much by way of response, the nurse taking it upon herself to answer for little Lizzybet.

Glancing back to the trees, she saw that all the adults were fully engaged, the gentlemen having disposed themselves on the blankets with the ladies. Having no desire to join them, Marianne persuaded herself she would not be missed. Moving to the other side of the Monument, she headed for a copse of trees a little distance away.

It was restful to lean against a convenient trunk, out of sight of the rest of the party, and at last allow herself to dwell on the earlier happenings of the morning.

She felt utterly drained, as if she had gone through hoops of emotion. Only now did she realise how Alex's questions had raked up the embers of distress she had carefully tamped down within herself. The rawness of the grief surprised her. Had she fooled herself into thinking she had managed to control it?

The desire to escape revived. Should she put into execution that scheme she'd spoken of to Alex, half in jest? Advertise for a husband? Who knew what kind of creature she might conjure up with such a project? How would she know if some seeming gentlemanly man would not turn out to be a brutal beast? And she would have put herself voluntarily at his mercy. Unthinkable. A loveless marriage to Justin had to be better than that.

"Do you object to it if I join you?"

Marianne jumped, her eyes flying open, her heart bumping with violence. "Good heavens, Justin, how you startled me!"

He did not smile. He was standing a couple of feet away, regarding her with a frown and troubled eyes. "Forgive me."

He spoke as if the words were perfunctory, his mind elsewhere.

Her heart had steadied, but the rhythm of Marianne's pulse became uneven. Her mind blanked. She could think of nothing whatsoever to say.

Justin drew a breath and sighed it out. "I owe you an apology. I mistook what I saw. I should not have — I had no right to…"

He looked away. Embarrassment? Marianne sought in vain for words to ease the strain. The chasm separating them seemed to widen.

Justin's frowning gaze came back to her. "Is it true you are planning to leave us?"

Us? No, Justin, it was he alone she was planning to leave. But she could not say so. She seized excuses from the air.

"My services are no longer needed."

"Your services?" Shock in his tone. "What of your companionship?"

"To whom? Grace has the Dragon now and Jocasta is soon to be married."

*As will you be all too soon.* She could not bring herself to say it. Yet Justin's face showed her he might as well have read the words written across her forehead.

"What you mean is, Marianne, you are leaving to escape me."

His tone was harsh, hurt rife within it.

Denial hovered on Marianne's lips. What came out of her mouth was not at all what she meant to say. "Justin, can you not see how impossible this is?"

"I can only see how impossible it will be if you go!"

She stared at him, hardly daring to breathe. Could it be she was mistaken? Did his feelings run deeper than she had supposed? But why should he not have said as much if that were so?

"Justin…"

He moved in, towards her, his eyes never leaving hers. The air closed in around her.

"Purford, there you are!"

Marianne shifted swiftly to one side, even as Justin wheeled to face Ibbotson, smiling a few yards away.

"Ah, and Miss Timperley too. We have settled it we should repair to an inn for refreshments. The children are missing a luncheon and I confess I am devilish sharp-set myself. Will you come?"

Never had a day seemed longer. The Ibbotsons, not content with the noisy party at The White Horse in Ripley — where a selection of viands was consumed along with lemonade for the ladies and flagons of ale for the gentlemen — must needs take it into their heads to return to Purford Park for the afternoon.

Though that was due to Jocasta's persuasions, conceded Marianne, trying to be fair. Harriet Ibbotson had jumped at the offer, however, squeaking with excitement.

"How dearly I should love to come, Jocasta. What a splendid notion! And we need not return to Send Place until the children's dinner hour. I declare, the very thought of Grandmama Bentinck's gloomy countenance is enough to make me wish to park myself upon you for a se'ennight."

Fortunately, since Grace looked nothing short of horrified, her spouse vetoed the suggestion in no uncertain terms.

"My dear Harriet, there can be no question of remaining away. It is kind of Lady Jocasta to invite us, but I think we would do better to go back to the Place directly."

A storm of protest greeted this, Grace loudest of all. Marianne guessed she felt guilty for her previous lapse of manners in showing her disquiet at a lengthy stay. Ibbotson perforce agreed to a short visit to Purford Park, but in the event the party remained until the children were dropping with fatigue, their parents having been persuaded to dine. Marianne arranged for the children to be fed and Mrs Woofferton assigned a bedchamber for their use.

Mrs Ibbotson exclaimed at finding it well past seven o'clock when the carriages were called for, since it was still light. Her husband and Lord Tazewell carried the yawning boys down, while the nurse managed a sleeping Lizzybet.

"Oh, only look at my precious little sleepyheads," cooed their mother, looking fondly upon them and dropping a kiss on each tousled child's cheek. "Such an adventurous day they've had, little dears. I know they will be enraptured forever with their Aunt Jocasta."

Tazewell coloured a little at this blatant pre-empting of his nuptials, but Jocasta let out a merry laugh.

"Well, they may be sure their Aunt Jocasta will be just as enraptured with them."

The farewells took an inordinate amount of time as the Purford party necessarily had to wait while the arrangement of half-asleep children was going forward. But at last Harriet Ibbotson leaned from the window to wave, calling out protestations of future meetings and a battery of thanks until the coach turned a corner so that her sight of the waving hosts must be curtailed.

Marianne could swear she heard a collective sigh of relief, and Grace turned instantly to Miss Stubbings, who had joined the party on their return to the Park.

"Pray ring for the tea tray at once, Amelia. I am quite as exhausted as those poor little children."

Lord Tazewell looked a little dismayed, but since Grace was already entering the house, he addressed himself to Justin. "I'm afraid my sister outstayed her welcome."

"Oh, nonsense, Tom," cut in Jocasta before her brother could respond. "It has been delightful. I love Harriet already, and I know we will become the greatest of friends."

Her betrothed smiled gratefully at her, and Marianne was relieved when Justin spoke up, albeit with what she recognised to be false joviality.

"You need have no apprehension, Tazewell. We have been very well entertained, and I am glad Jocasta had this opportunity to become acquainted with your sister and her family. Shall we go in?"

Jocasta drew Tazewell forward, whispering in his ear, and Marianne made haste to follow. Just as she crossed the threshold, she overheard Alex, who was behind with Justin.

"Doing it a trifle too brown, old fellow. Don't tell me you ain't on the fidgets, coz, for I know you better than that."

Justin was not the only one, Marianne reflected, as she crossed the hall and entered the parlour where tea was to be served. To use Alex's expression, she'd been on the fidgets the entire day, unable to focus, her mind jumping with questions every moment she was not occupied with organisation or responding to the general discussion.

Fortunately, Jocasta and Grace had taken the brunt of Harriet Ibbotson's discourse, which left Justin to entertain her spouse and Tazewell, ably supported by Lord Dymond. It did not help Marianne in the least. When the gentlemen were off somewhere else, her thoughts dwelled obstinately on the snatch of a meeting in the copse she'd had with Justin. When they re-joined the ladies, she was unable to think at all, her unruly pulses thrumming to his presence, her attention pulled to him whether or not he was in her line of sight.

On tenterhooks, she could not but be aware that Justin was equally conscious. She caught him watching her several times, whipping her eyes away when she met his glance, her breath instantly short, her heart jerking uncontrollably.

By the time tea was served, Marianne was as much exhausted by the disorder of her senses as the lengthy period of entertaining the visitors. She was inordinately relieved when the Dragon took it upon herself to dispense tea, leaving her free of the necessity to concentrate.

Only Tazewell and Jocasta, engaged in muted talk, were animated. Lying back in her chair in an attitude suggestive of immediate collapse, Grace sipped at intervals with an obvious effort. Justin began by prowling and then came to rest leaning his back against the mantelpiece. But Alex, who brought Marianne's tea over, took a seat beside her.

"Been hoping for a word with you."

Wary, she eyed him. "About this morning?"

"That's it. Shouldn't have taken snuff, even though my idiot coz did as much. Silly thing to do. Quite right to take us both to task."

Amusement lifted Marianne's mood. "I admit I felt rather like a nursemaid at the time."

A barked guffaw from Alex caused Justin to turn his head to look at them both. Heat stung Marianne's cheeks and she took refuge in her tea cup.

"Thing is, Marianne," pursued Alex, low-voiced, "I might have given you away. Didn't mean to, but I had to say something."

Deep foreboding gripped her. "What exactly did you say?"

He looked rueful. "Not what you'd be pardoned for imagining. Didn't betray your confidence. But he's pretty sharp, is my cousin Justin. Might have added two and two to make four."

Her heart thrumming all over again, Marianne could not resist a look at Justin, but his attention was once more concentrated on the empty grate as he drank his tea.

"Just what did you say, Alex? Be plain with me, I implore you."

"Only told him you'd embraced this notion of my mother's, to find yourself a husband."

"He said he'd heard I was leaving."

"Well, yes, I told him that too. Said you wanted to leave, and marriage was the only way."

Shocked disappointment flooded Marianne. No wonder Justin had taxed her with it! Of course he would do so, and no doubt meant to renew his suggestion that she married him rather than look elsewhere. He must feel obligated, responsible for her welfare. She must acknowledge he cared enough for that. What a fool she was to dare to hope his coming after her, questioning her, meant more.

The drop, after a day of anxiety she now recognised to be rooted in desperate hope, proved too great.

"Excuse me, if you please, Alex. I am — I am much too tired to think straight. I must go to bed."

She rose on the words, crossing to set down her cup and saucer. She kept her eyes firmly away from Justin, and addressed herself to her cousin.

"I am going to retire, Grace. Forgive me, but I cannot remain awake any longer."

"Oh, I shall be right behind you, Marianne. I am quite drained. Such a pleasant couple, but it has been a long day."

The last was added with a nod and a smile towards Tazewell, and Marianne seized the chance to say a quick goodnight in the direction of the engaged couple, which sufficiently included Justin for her to able to avoid looking directly at him.

Her heart full to bursting, she managed to reach the door in as nonchalant a fashion as she could. Once outside, she flew up the stairs, but the tears were already falling by the time she reached the safety of her bedchamber.

# Chapter Eighteen

Justin watched Marianne's exit with dismay, bewilderment wreathing his brain. He crossed to his cousin and took her vacated chair.

"What the deuce did you say to her?"

Alex's mobile brows rose. "Nothing untoward, coz. Had to smooth things over, that's all."

"Then why did she run off like that?"

His cousin shrugged. "Said she was tired. Couldn't keep her eyes open. Don't blame her. Devilish day. I'm minded to turn in myself."

Justin gave him a glare, muttering almost under his breath. "No, you don't. I'm not entertaining Tazewell on my own, so don't think it."

Alex glanced across to where the betrothed couple still had their heads together. "He might want an early night, for all you know."

"Not he. Haven't you learned yet how punctilious the fellow is? He'll think he has a duty to me as his host to remain and take a glass of brandy."

His prediction was proven a few moments later when Grace called to Jocasta to come upstairs. Of course she could not be permitted to remain unchaperoned. He sighed as the two ladies, accompanied by Miss Stubbings, left the room and Tazewell turned to him with an apologetic smile.

"I feel I ought to beg your pardon once again, Purford. I might have known my sister wouldn't leave when she was deriving so much pleasure from being here."

Justin moved to the bell-pull and tugged on it, dredging up what patience he could find to resume his duty as host. "I am glad Mrs Ibbotson enjoyed her stay. No apologies are necessary. Your sister and her family have become quite a part of ours, which is all to the good, don't you think?"

Tazewell laughed, though he flushed too. "Very good of you to say so, Purford."

"I wish you will call me Justin. It is ridiculous to maintain formality under the circumstances."

The flush in the fellow's cheeks deepened. He really was excessively self-effacing. Justin was inclined to think it a miracle the man had taken his flighty sister's fancy.

The door opened and his butler appeared in the aperture, accompanied by a minion armed with a tray, upon which reposed a decanter and three glasses.

"Ah, you've anticipated our need, Rowsham. I thank you."

Alex asked Tazewell some question about his brother-in-law's estate, relieving Justin of the necessity to make polite conversation while the servants were in the room. Presently, with the tea-tray removed, the brandy poured and served, he was able to usher his guest and cousin to seats either side of the fireplace — innocent of any fire in the height of summer — and draw up a chair for himself next to Tazewell.

"Well, Tom, if I may —?"

"Oh, of course, sir, if informality is to be the order of the day."

Not that the fellow seemed able to be informal himself. Justin felt as if the few years between them were nearer ten or fifteen.

"I was going to ask if you have hit upon a date for the wedding."

For want of anything else he could think of. But this Justin kept to himself. He could have cursed. The last thing he wished to discuss was the vexed subject of weddings.

"Well, Jocasta has consented to a date this year, which pleases me. At first she was adamant we should wait. Why she changed her mind, I know not, but I'm happy to think she is so eager."

Was he deluded? Justin could not judge of the depth of his sister's feelings, though from his observation the couple had drawn closer through these weeks. A source of unrest to him, since his own situation was unsatisfactory, to say the least.

He came out of this brief reverie to find his cousin had taken the conversation in a different direction, drawing Tazewell to talk of his stable and hunting. An innocuous subject that lasted long enough to enable the obligatory session to come to an end before Justin was driven to the edge of frustration.

At last Tazewell yawned, flushed, apologised and laughed. "I must be more tired than I knew. If you will forgive me, Justin, I think I will take to my bed."

Nothing could have pleased him more, and as he made the necessary offers of more brandy — and then, when this was refused, a candle from the selection awaiting the gentlemen on the table in the hall where a footman was ready with a taper — he managed a glance at his cousin which he tried to invest with a message to him to remain behind.

It was successful, for the moment the door closed behind Tazewell, Lord Dymond poured another half inch of the golden liquid in the decanter into his glass and turned back to Justin.

"What's to do, coz?"

Justin sighed. "I don't really know, Alex. I've never known a longer day. I feel as if I've been to hell and back."

His cousin laughed. "Know what you mean. Myself I'd have called it purgatory. Good enough fellow, Ibbotson, but doing the pretty for hours on end is enough to try anyone."

"It isn't that. Except inasmuch as their presence kept me too much occupied."

Alex subjected him to a long look. "Still in the hips, coz? Told you there was nothing in it. Don't you believe me?"

For an instant, an echo of the molten rage that had enveloped him at finding Marianne in his cousin's arms crept back. He suppressed it as best he could.

"I do believe you. What irks me is why Marianne needed comfort."

"Well, you ain't expecting me to betray her, are you? What do you take me for?"

Justin threw up a hand. "There's no need to fly up into the boughs. I know you would not. But allow me the curiosity to wonder."

Alex's jaw was tight. "Wonder no longer, coz. Didn't concern you. Weren't mentioned, except when she said she meant to try and marry elsewhere. And I shouldn't have told you that either."

Disregarding the note of remorse, Justin stared at his cousin. "What do you mean? How was I mentioned?"

"Damn it, Justin, don't ask me!"

"Alex, for heaven's sake! Can't you see I'm going crazy?"

Alex let out a grunt. "Well, if you must have it, it was me. So shocked by what she said, I told her she ought to marry you if she was set on a marriage of convenience. However, she wouldn't have that at any price."

The blow hit hard. He'd been coxcomb enough to think Marianne's distress signalled a change of heart. His memory flew to the moments he'd stolen to waylay her in the trees. For an instant he'd been sure she cared. Had he been about to kiss her? He hardly knew now what his intention had been. If Ibbotson had not interrupted them, Lord knows what might have transpired.

All day he'd relived the change he thought he'd detected. Had he been mistaken? Had he built a castle on a false premise? How, when he'd seen it in her eyes? And Marianne had been as conscious, he'd swear to that. Protest rose up.

"If that's true, why did she rush out in distress tonight?"

He was hardly aware of speaking aloud. Alexander's voice startled him.

"I told you. She was tired."

Justin smote his knee with one fist. "No, it was more than that. I don't care what she said to you this morning. When I spoke to her at that cursed Monument…"

He faded out, unwilling to share a conviction that Alex might feel compelled to quash. If he'd given his word to Marianne, he was honour bound and must keep it. But Justin could not rid himself of the suspicion that the comfort Alex had administered had everything to do with him. Why else would she be seeking to escape?

And that was a nonsense. At least he could put a stop to that.

Alex rose and set down his glass. Justin found himself under scrutiny and frowned.

"What? Why do you look at me so?"

His cousin shifted his shoulders. "Just thinking. Must be devilish to be in Marianne's shoes. Hadn't considered before, but only think. No means of her own. No family besides yours. Wholly dependent on Lady Purford's charity. Which is to say, wholly dependent on you, coz."

The awful truth of this swept into Justin's heart. Marianne had ever been so much a member of the family, he had not stopped to think of how humiliating her position must be. But Alex had not finished.

"Thing is, coz, there ain't much choice for a girl in her condition. She can't leave, however much she wants to. Spoke of hiring herself out for a companion or some such, but Marianne knew well you'd not stand for that."

"Good God, no!"

Appalled, Justin could only be glad Marianne had not mentioned that suggestion to him. He would have gone through the roof and she must have known it.

"Don't suppose Lady Purford would support her in that notion either, though I take it all's not been well between the two of them of late."

Justin had not realised this either. He knew there had been a falling out, but he'd thought matters had improved since he installed the Dragon in Marianne's place. He'd hoped to relieve her of some of her burdens, if he could do nothing else for her.

"Truth is, coz, marriage is the only way out."

Bitterness gnawed at Justin. "And marriage with me being unacceptable to her, she wants to flee my vicinity. Yes, the irony does not escape me, Alex."

To his confusion, his cousin broke into a grin. "Exactly so, old fellow. Only one thing for you to do, ain't there?"

# Chapter Nineteen

Waking with a heavy head only when Nancy drew back the curtains around her bed, Marianne screwed her eyes into slits against the light.

"I've brought your chocolate, Miss Marianne."

She blinked owlishly at the maid, whose eyes popped at her. A lively girl, who had long served Marianne as well as the Dragon, leaving Ellen free for her duties towards the more important members of the household, she made no bones about speaking her mind.

"Goodness, miss, you do look awful peaky! Are you ill? 'Tisn't like you to sleep so late neither."

Marianne struggled to sit up, feeling a rush of pain about her forehead.

"Dearie me! Here, let me."

Nancy plumped and banked the pillows behind her, and Marianne sank against them in relief, letting her head fall back.

The maid eyed her, clucking concern. "Seems to me as if I ought to fetch Mrs Woofferton to you, Miss Marianne."

"No, Nancy, no need. I am not ill. I didn't sleep well, that's all."

"Yes, and anyone could see that," said the girl in a scolding tone, as she reached for the cup reposing on a tray by the bed and lifted off the lid.

A welcome aroma wafted into Marianne's nostrils and she took the cup in a shaky grasp, sipping gratefully at the sweet hot liquid inside.

Nancy beamed. "There, that's doing you good, isn't it? Mrs Woofferton always says there's nothing like a cup of chocolate to put heart into a body."

Marianne managed a smile. "She's right. I'll be better presently."

The maid frowned. "Well, don't you be hurrying to get up, Miss Marianne. You stay there and take your rest for once."

Well aware the female staff jealously guarded her welfare, apparently believing her to be put-upon by Grace, Marianne let this pass without comment.

"Am I very late? What is the time, Nancy?"

"It's gone nine, miss."

Marianne almost dropped the cup. "Gone nine? Good heavens, why did you not wake me earlier?"

"Mrs Woofferton told me not to. She said you were looking tired out yesterday."

Oh, dear Lord! How many others had noticed how distrait she'd been? She must strive for more control.

"Would you fetch up my hot water, if you please, Nancy? Stay! Is — is anyone else up already?"

The girl paused on her way to the door and came back again.

"His lordship and Lord Dymond have gone riding, but the other gentleman and Lady Jocasta ain't been seen yet. Her ladyship is still abed. Ellen didn't like to wake her neither."

That was one mercy. And if she hurried, she could take breakfast before Alex and Justin came in. They would be obliged to change their clothes before breaking their fast. This determined, she addressed the maid, who was still hovering.

"Thank you, Nancy. Pray fetch up the water directly."

The fuzziness in her head receded as she drank her chocolate and waited for the maid to return with her large porcelain jug filled with hot water. It did not take her long to wash and dress herself in her thick muslin workaday gown, and she took a moment to confer with Mrs Woofferton before entering the breakfast parlour.

Only Miss Stubbings was present, as ever prim in her everlasting supply of plain chintz gowns in fusty colours. She was just finishing her repast, and Marianne found it easy enough to respond to a series of desultory remarks about the prettiness of Harriet Ibbotson, the excellent manners of her spouse and how Grace had doted on the children.

Her mind was far from yesterday's visitors. With the flurry of preparation over, she could not prevent her thoughts returning, as she consumed a light meal of rolls and coffee, to the pangs of a dismal and sleepless night.

She'd allowed herself the luxury of weeping into her pillows for a time. It was not her custom to succumb to such weakness, and she despised herself for her lack of control. But the lowness of spirits pursued her into her dreams when she at last fell asleep, treacherously presenting her with the age-old visions of being held in Justin's arms, of being loved and cherished by him in the way she'd longed for almost since the day they'd met.

Her immature fancy had deepened as she grew to womanhood, and their friendship gave her an intimate knowledge of his character. Her affections became fixed and the dreams ripened. But she'd not had them for some time and could only suppose they'd been conjured by yesterday's events.

Miss Stubbings soon left, declaring she must go and see to Grace's comfort, and Marianne was able to drink a second cup of coffee in peace.

Her thoughts drifted, numbed by the aftermath of an uncomfortable night.

It seemed an age since the appalling scandal of Lady Selina's escape. Almost as though it had happened to some other family. So much had changed. She ought to be grateful to Tazewell, whose offer had lifted them into celebration after the plunging disaster.

Marianne was struck all at once by the oddity of the last few weeks. A year ago, she would have given anything to be in the situation she was in now. Nor would she have hesitated if Justin had asked her then to marry him. How strange it was that the opportunity she'd longed for should have cast her into a pool of dejection.

Had she been foolish? She'd bayed for the moon, instead of being content with a sprinkling of stars. It was too late now. Too much damage had been done. But what if she'd accepted him at the outset?

A swift review of their relationship since was enough to convince her she had done right. How pitiful must her situation be now had she agreed to marry him. To be intimate without the intimacy of mutual affection? No. She would be in as much turmoil as she now was, if not worse. Because she'd have no means to extricate herself once she'd committed to the marriage.

At least now she had a choice. A new determination buoyed her. She would write to Lady Luthrie and throw herself upon that lady's mercy.

Deciding what she must do served to settle her mind. Meanwhile, she had duties to attend to. She found herself at once thinking of how she could arrange for the various tasks she undertook to be apportioned to others. Much of what she did could be undertaken by Miss Stubbings. Grace might not like it, but she must bestir herself to do more. And some few things would need to pass back to Justin, or his agent. There could be no difficulty. No one person was indispensable. Marianne could readily be replaced.

She was able to continue in this frame of mind for some little while, but it proved less efficacious than she had hoped. Each action she performed felt like a pinprick of loss, as if she mentally said farewell to her unofficial stance as mistress of the household. The realisation of how closely interwoven she was in Justin's life, by virtue of what she did to ensure the smooth running of his home, could not but pierce the thin armour she'd erected around her misery.

A reminder from Mrs Woofferton completed her discomfiture.

"That Peggy Baker is still unwell, Miss Marianne, though she sent to ask if we've work for her to do. I was wondering if I should let her have a little darning. Those sheets we looked out t'other day need doing, and she could manage that. It'd relieve you and Lady Jocasta of all that sewing too."

Marianne agreed to it, adding that she would try to visit Peggy again. She wondered briefly if Grace might be persuaded to go, and dismissed the thought at once. Grace would never enter a cottage where she might be subject to catching some illness, convinced she was susceptible to infection.

"Such a pity about those curtains, miss. The women worked hard to finish them. Seems a shame they'll go to waste."

Startled, Marianne stared at her. "Go to waste? Why should they?"

"Well, you said at the time it was a makeshift solution. I dare say, when his lordship chooses another, the new mistress won't be satisfied."

Her mind all chaos, Marianne knew not how she replied. Another mistress? Some unknown female to discard those beautiful curtains? To throw her choice aside, as of no account? A hectic mix of emotions churned within her.

Excusing herself to the housekeeper, she sped up the stairs and into the gallery that led to the principal rooms.

Standing in the bedchamber adjoining Justin's, Marianne's gaze fell upon the golden coverlet and swiftly shifted to the tied curtains, held at each post so that a fall of the material showed the exquisite pattern of birds, twine and leaves.

Moving forward, Marianne set her fingers on the pattern, tracing the birds one by one, moving around the post to which the curtain was fixed, her mind alive with memories once again.

Without warning, the hidden well of distress came gushing up to claim her.

Struggling for control and finding her knees weak, she sank onto the golden coverlet, letting her hands fall. Without will her touch ran across the silky sheen as she fought the pricking tears. She must not give way. This was merely the effect of nostalgia. A snippet of her life only was in these curtains, this coverlet. Ridiculous to allow them to conquer her when her determination was fixed.

Her throat ached with holding back the threatening grief, a leaden weight in her chest.

A scrape of sound shot question into her head, suspending the distressing symptoms within her. Gaining focus as she looked up, she saw the door to Justin's apartment opening.

Panic threw her to her feet as he appeared in the aperture. He stopped dead.

"Marianne!"

Before she could react, he closed the door, moving towards her.

"I've been searching for you all over! Why in the world are you hiding in here?"

Marianne's tongue froze. Must he take it into his head to come looking for her just at this moment?

In seconds he was close enough to see her properly and his face changed.

"What is it?"

His instant recognition of her state wrought havoc within her. The need to conceal it dictated her tone. "Nothing! What do you want, Justin?"

Those green eyes fairly glared into hers. With a jolt, Marianne recognised the stubborn tilt to his chin.

"Don't fob me off! I know you are distressed. You were last night when you ran away."

"I didn't run away!"

"You did, and you've been crying!"

"I have not!"

"Don't dare lie to me, for I know you too well."

Marianne's temper got the better of her. "Oh, be quiet! Have you not plagued me enough?"

Justin grasped her unwilling hands, holding them hard. "Marianne, listen to me! You are not leaving this house, do you understand me?"

From nowhere, rage climbed into Marianne's bosom. She wrenched her hands away, springing away from him towards the head of the bed.

"How dare you dictate to me? Am I your chattel, your slave, that you can order my movements as you choose?"

He came after her, seizing her shoulders. "Neither, and that's just the point. No, don't try to escape me. You will listen!"

"Justin, let me go, or by heaven —"

He gave her a shake and Marianne threw him a fulminating look. Useless to struggle. Instead, she went rigid under his hands.

"Go on then if you must."

"Don't say it like that!" His tone softened. "Marianne, I can't let you go, you must see that. It touches my honour, apart from anything else."

Despite the fury, Marianne's acute common sense saw the force of this. "You need not spell it out. I am all too aware of my situation."

"Yes, but I don't think you are."

Resentment sprang up and she pushed at his wrists. "Release me, Justin."

"I'm not letting you go until you see sense. I've been too easy with you, Marianne."

"Easy!"

"Yes. I've allowed your nonsensical scruples to weigh with me, but since you insist on behaving like a lunatic, I've made up my mind not to do so any longer."

"And I've made up my mind to do exactly as I choose!"

Justin's hold tightened, and his tone became urgent. "Then choose to marry me, Marianne. For God's sake, stop being so utterly proud and imprudent! It's not as if I don't love you!"

The world went still. Marianne's burgeoning anger slid out of her grasp. For a moment of wild confusion, she thought she was asleep and dreaming again. Her brain began to whirl and she swayed.

"I think I'm going to faint."

Justin's hands abruptly left her shoulders, and he caught her instead. "Dear Lord! Here, sit down."

She found herself on the bed, one hand clinging to a post, the other pushed down into the coverlet as she fought to maintain her balance. Her head slowly cleared. She looked up to find Justin watching her in some concern.

Anxiety gnawed at her. She must know!

"What did you say?"

It came out a near whisper, and Marianne held her breath as he frowned.

"When?"

"Just now. You said…"

He shrugged, as if the matter was of no account. "I don't know. I said you should marry me."

To her own bewilderment, Marianne felt the fury reviving. The words were out before she could stop them. "No, not that! You said you loved me. Didn't you say that? Did you?"

He threw out his hands in a gesture utterly confused. "Yes, but why are you angry?"

She paid no heed to this. "You love me?"

He flushed. "I beg your pardon if it upsets you, but yes, I love you. I've always loved you."

She was on her feet, rage burning through her even as tears began to trickle down her cheeks. "You idiot man!" Balling a fist, she hit Justin in the chest. "Stupid, idiot creature! Why could you not have said so before?"

He caught her wrists before she could strike him again, urgency in his voice. "Wait! Wait! Before you ring your peal over me, why, Marianne? Why are you angry when I tell you that I love you?"

She wrenched her hands away, dashing at her cheeks, hardly able to get the words out. "Why do you — do you think, you — you — oh, I could cheerfully take an axe to you, you unfeeling, pitiless —"

"For God's sake, *why?*"

"B-because you b-broke my h-heart!"

200

Light entered his features, and he caught her face between his hands, the green eyes tender. "Oh, my love, don't weep! I never meant to hurt you."

"But you did, Justin, you did! For y-years you've had all my h-heart. How could you not know that?"

A faint smile flickered, and his eyes shone. His voice was unsteady. "Because I'm an idiot, Marianne, just as you said."

A watery chuckle escaped her and she did not resist when he drew her into his arms. She rested her head against his shoulder, catching her breath as the desire to weep began to recede.

For a long moment, Justin did not move, and Marianne was content to be held, to feel his warmth, his strength and his love, to be where she'd longed to be. A glow, like a tiny candle, began in her breast, seeping through her whole being, warming the cold places she'd harboured for too many years.

At last the embrace loosened, and she raised her head and met his eyes, so close, intense with something that sent a fleeting thrill along her veins. Her thoughts became suspended. An eon passed.

She felt his fingers on her chin, and one tip ran briefly across her lips, sending a flitter of warmth pursuing the thrill. She could not breathe as his face came closer. The veriest touch of his lips on hers — tentative, like a butterfly. The kiss, like nothing she had ever dreamed, was magical. Soft, tender, replete with affection.

And then it changed. Justin's hold about her tightened, his mouth pressed closer, harder, and she heard his intake of breath even as heat seared her insides.

Involuntarily she gave a soft moan. As if it was a flame to tinder, Justin responded with a groan, dragging her so close against him she could feel every muscle in his chest, the hardness of his legs even through her petticoats. The sheer manliness of his form drove her brain into frenzy.

Aware of nothing save sensation, Marianne returned the assault with fervour, until Justin pulled away, breathing hard and staring down at her with dismay and shock in his eyes.

"We had best get married right away!"

Marianne, both mind and body tousled into confusion, began to laugh. "Wretched creature! Have you no sense of romance?"

Justin broke into a grin and caught her briefly against him. "My God, but I adore you!" He put her from him, his hands firm. "Let us damp things down before I dare touch you again."

He let her go, and Marianne, suddenly weak at the knees, groped for the bed and sank down upon it.

"Not the most uninviting position you could assume," Justin said, with a wry look.

A gurgle of laughter escaped her. "It's your fault. You've made me feel as if my bones are made of marchpane."

He laughed, but caught her hand and made to pull her up. "We'll continue this conversation elsewhere, I think."

"Just give me a moment to recover, if you please."

He did not let go of her hand, instead holding it in both his own, caressing her skin in a way that made her veins hum in an echo of the earlier eruption.

Gradually her mind cleared, and the happenings of the last few minutes replayed in her head. Catching on his words, a flicker of puzzlement crept in. She did not hesitate.

"But, Justin, why didn't you say it? When Jocasta made that dreadful faux pas and you threw your offer at me."

"I didn't throw it at you!" The indignant look abated and a wry smile came. "Well, perhaps I did. But it wasn't out of the blue."

"It seemed so to me. Or no, that isn't the truth either."

Justin sat on the bed, careful to leave a little space between them, but retained his clasp on her hand. "What is the truth, Marianne? There's been so much confusion and upset, I scarcely know myself."

"I know, my dearest. Oh, I know."

His chest swelled at the endearment, the tenderness of the sound. Almost he caught her back into his embrace, but prudence won. He loved her too dearly to risk losing control. He had hurt her too much already. Monstrous to cheat the marriage bed and bring her to ruin before he'd pledged himself to her, body and soul.

Her dear eyes were warm as they looked into his, but rueful.

"I'm afraid I thought of marriage with you the moment I heard about Selina's defection."

Shock enveloped him. "Then? But for pity's sake, Marianne, couldn't you see I had the self-same thought?"

A disbelieving laugh escaped her. "How would I? You were wounded. Oh, I knew you didn't care for her, even before you told me so. But she hurt you nonetheless."

It seemed so long since he'd felt anything at all about the debacle with Selina that the whole notion was alien. "Well, if you want the truth, I spent far more time agonizing over whether to seize my chance with you than I did over Selina."

Marianne's lips twitched and she erupted into giggles. Confused, Justin let go of her hand.

"Now what?"

"It's — it's ridiculous! The — the both of us, agonizing over — over whether to ask each other, and all the time…"

Enlightenment dawned. "Do you mean to tell me you thought of asking me?"

Her giggles ceased, but her eyes were bright with laughter and tears both. "Yes! Highly improper, but I was so afraid some horrid designing female would snatch you up. Only I found I couldn't do it."

His heart cracked with the poignancy of it all, but he could not let it pass. "And after all that, you rejected me? I don't know what you deserve." Unholy glee entered his breast. "Oh, yes, I do, though."

He wiggled his fingers experimentally, daring her to object.

"Justin, no!"

"Marianne, yes!"

This time he was not deterred. He began tickling her, just where he knew she was most vulnerable. Marianne wriggled, protesting, but he refused to have mercy.

"Stop it! Justin, don't!"

But she was giggling all over again and the delight the sound engendered in him spurred him on. He could not help laughing, feeling all the release of the pent-up frustrations of the past days.

Marianne, helpless with breathless merriment, unable to stop Justin's merciless assault, lost all ability to control her limbs. She found herself down on the bed with Justin half on top of her. The compromising nature of the position came home to her all at once and she stilled, even as he did, evidently struck by the same realisation.

The air in the room seemed to vanish. There was a moment of hectic suspension as she gazed into the rising heat in Justin's eyes.

He kissed her again. A convulsive meeting of lip to lip that touched something explosive within her. She knew from his response that Justin felt it too.

He came up for air and groaned her name. *"Marianne."*

Her eyes opening, she met his heated gaze and the weight of years fell away from her heart. She brought one hand up and touched his face.

"I've loved you since the moment you leapt off your horse and came to my rescue."

His smile embraced her. "And I, most improperly, loved you back."

"Even then?"

"All too soon."

Becoming aware of what he was doing, Justin abruptly threw himself off her and leaned to drag her up. "This won't do. Any more and I'll be tempted beyond my capacity to withstand you." To his tender amusement, she blushed like a girl. Justin had to laugh. "My darling, don't be conscious. You've no notion how many times I've almost given in to the overmastering desire to kiss you."

"You don't mean it?"

"Do I look as if I don't mean it?" He gestured at his dishevelled neck-cloth and the disarray of his costume, feeling all the discomfort of his arousal. "You've been seductive since you were about sixteen."

Her mouth fell ludicrously open. "I have not. I don't believe you."

With determination, he forced himself to his feet and dragged her up. "Don't expect me to demonstrate again, because I won't be able to stop."

"I never knew I had such power over you."

"Marianne, you've had power over me from the first moment of my setting eyes on you. You've been a thorn in my flesh and a source of agony of mind forever."

This confession could not but warm her. Marianne thrilled to the knowledge of his passion, for his words echoed her own experience and she did not doubt him for a moment.

"Come, we'll go and break the news." He led her towards the door, and then halted, turning back to frown at her. "What am I thinking? You haven't yet said you will marry me."

Mischief flitted across her face. "You haven't yet asked me."

"I've asked you about three times, probably more. But I'll ask you again." His eyes softened and he caught her into his arms again. "Marianne, I love you. Will you please be my wife?"

Her eyes became luminous, her voice husky. "Yes, Justin, with all my heart."

This time, the kiss was tender, containing more of affection than Marianne could have wished. When he released her and would have resumed leaving the room, she stopped him.

"I think, you know, that we had both of us better effect some much needed repairs before showing ourselves."

He grinned. "What would I do without you, Miss Practicality?"

# Chapter Twenty

Jocasta, encountered in the hall as she emerged from the breakfast parlour in company with her betrothed after a belated repast, was ecstatic.

"I knew it, I knew it," she cried, subjecting her brother to a ruthless hug. "After you were so horrid to me too!"

Releasing Justin, she flung herself upon Marianne instead, who submitted, laughing, but protesting her ribs were being crushed.

"Well, it serves you right for taking so long about it," declared Jocasta, releasing her and seizing her hands. Tears stood in the girl's eyes and Marianne was touched. "My dearest, dearest Marianne, I could not be more happy! Now I shall have you for my real big sister, just as you've ever been to me."

Her effusions took some time, but Marianne interrupted them at last.

"Where is Grace, do you know?"

Jocasta made a face of comical dismay. "Oh, dear! Mama is going to go wild!"

"Jocasta!" Justin threw a glance at Tazewell and his sister blushed.

"Oh, I am sorry, don't scold. But Tom knows all about it, and he's very discreet. Besides, he is one of the family now."

Tazewell cleared his throat. "Jocasta, perhaps we should…?"

"Make ourselves scarce, you mean? Oh, very well. Unless you wish me to come with you for moral support, Marianne?"

Subduing the riffle of unease, Marianne thanked her but declined. "Where is she?"

"She said she was going to her parlour. On second thoughts, I think I won't come with you, for the Dragon is bound to be there."

Justin took Marianne's hand. "That is all to the good. Grace may pour her disapproval into the Dragon's ears and we need not stay to hear it."

As they ascended the stairs, Justin tried to comfort her, squeezing the hand he held.

"Don't fret, my love. She can do nothing to put a bar in our way."

Marianne's insides fluttered. "But she won't like it. I know she doesn't want me to marry you."

"Or anyone, if we are to judge by her outburst that day."

He sounded grim and Marianne halted on the landing, turning to him as the flutter built to something akin to panic.

"Exactly so, Justin. She has been distant with me ever since. I do feel for her in this. I know it must be galling to her to think of my supplanting her as mistress here."

Justin all but snorted. "That's rich! You supplanted her in all but name years ago, and she knows it. She encouraged it, and it suited her very well indeed."

Marianne put a finger to his lips. "Oh, hush, Justin. Only think. If she had not brought me here and given me a home —
"

"For which you've repaid her a thousandfold and with scant reward!"

"No, don't say that, for it isn't true. She's been kind and loving to me all these years. It was only since…"

"Since my good aunt began trying to get you married off, yes."

Marianne shook his hand roughly. "Oh, stop, my dearest one, and listen to me. What I meant to say is that without

Grace's charity, I should never have met you, and that does not bear thinking of."

Justin's mouth quirked and his eyes teased. "I'll remember to thank her."

"Don't you dare!" She sighed, and urged him onward. "We had best get it over with."

Grace was discovered in animated discussion with Miss Stubbings, the two of them poring over a periodical depicting the latest fashions. She looked up as Marianne entered the room with Justin right behind her, and it was immediately apparent that Grace had divined their errand.

The matron's eyes went from one to the other. As if she took in something from their faces, her gaze registered horror and she let fall a soft "Oh, no!"

Justin, taking the bull by the horns, grabbed Marianne's hand and led her forward.

"Grace, we've come to tell you we are going to be married."

Marianne's heart thumped painfully as her cousin's inimical gaze shifted from Justin's face to her own. Without will, she looked away, catching a satisfied look on the Dragon's face, which startled her. Was she pleased then? Oh, of course she was, for her situation with Grace must be secured.

Bracing herself for what her cousin would say, Marianne forced her eyes back. However, Grace was no longer looking at her, but at Justin, with a mix of anger and dismay.

"How could you, Justin? Will you go against your sainted Papa's expressed prohibition?"

Shock swept through Marianne. Without pausing for Justin's answer, she turned to him. "Is that true?"

His hand tightened on hers. "Perfectly true. When you were seventeen, and at last old enough, I told him I meant to make you my wife."

A radiant glow swept through Marianne. All this time! And she'd thought he didn't care. Her eyes filled. "Oh, Justin!"

He brought her hand to his lips and kissed it. "I should have defied him then. I wish I had."

Oblivious to her audience, Marianne set her hands to his shoulders. "I thought you were going to offer for me when I turned eighteen. I expected it. And when you didn't…"

His fingers came up to her cheeks, wiping away the trace of moisture.

"Believe me, I suffered as much as you did. Only my father caused me to believe I owed a duty to Selina."

"Yes, that is what Grace told me. That you were promised to her."

Grace's shrill tones cut in. "Which was perfectly true. At least I spared you the knowledge that my husband did not consider you good enough for his son."

"Grace!"

Leaving Marianne, Justin turned on his stepmother, who ignored him.

"He was heir to this earldom. He could not be permitted to throw himself away on a nobody like you."

"Grace, that will do! I will not have you speak to Marianne in that fashion."

"Justin, don't." Marianne left him and moved to her cousin, taking a chair beside her. "It's true, Grace. In birth, I am far beneath him."

"What the deuce does that matter?"

"Hush, Justin, pray. Grace, please try to understand. Justin did his duty by his father, in spite of our affection for one another. But with Lady Selina's elopement —"

"He was free and so you thought you would seize your chance."

"Nothing of the sort, Grace," Justin threw in furiously. "I took my chance, but she rejected me."

Marianne gestured for him to be patient. "I would have done just that, Grace. I very nearly did. But my courage failed me because I had been brought to believe Justin did not care for me. At least, not in the way of marriage. But it wasn't so."

Grace's features remained stubbornly tight, her chin high. "I little thought you would serve me a backhanded turn, Marianne. After all I've done for you."

Justin looked ready to explode, but Marianne again hushed him.

"I dare say it seems to you that I am doing so, but I promise you this will make little difference in your life."

Grace's eyes flared. "How dare you pretend? We cannot go on as we are. I might as well repair to the Dower House at once."

"That is your choice, but it's not what I meant."

"No doubt you'll expect it!"

Justin strode forward. "Oh, for pity's sake, Grace!"

"Justin, have patience!"

His glance swept to Marianne's and she sent him a pleading look. His jaw tightened, but he gave in to the silent message and relaxed back. She turned again to her cousin.

"This cannot change my regard for you, Grace."

She did not soften. "Don't speak of your regard for me. If you had any at all, you would not be stealing a march upon my daughter."

Taken aback, Marianne stared at her. "What in the world do you mean?"

"Are you stupid as well as unkind? Justin's nuptials must eclipse Jocasta's, of course."

Marianne fairly gasped. "Is that all?"

"If that is what troubles you, Grace, think nothing of it," said Justin. "We are going to be married swiftly and as quietly as we can contrive."

Grace looked aghast at this. "But why such unseemly haste? People will talk!"

"I've become accustomed to that, and Marianne will be subjected to far less impertinence if people must talk to the Countess of Purford rather than Miss Timperley."

This remark, while it could not but gratify Marianne, served to revive Grace's grievance.

"Countess of Purford indeed! If I did not know you better, Marianne, I would stigmatize you for a scheming wretch."

"But you do know me better, Grace," said Marianne, seizing on this. "In the eyes of the world, Justin will be thought to be marrying beneath him, but you, of all people, know better. Did not Lord Purford himself, if I may be so bold, marry you for love?"

The implication was clear enough. Grace's colour rose and she shifted in the way she had that signified discomfort, fiddling with her petticoats. "The cases are not the same."

Which was unarguable. Marianne sighed in defeat and rose. Justin took her hand again and drew her to the door, turning one last time to Grace.

"Pray don't show your displeasure too freely, Grace. At least pretend to be glad in public, for all our sakes."

As he closed the door behind him, Marianne remembered the presence of the Dragon.

"Dear heaven, we've been so indiscreet! I only hope Miss Stubbings is to be trusted not to spread all that about."

"Let her. There is bound to be talk, whatever we do."

"I suppose that is true. It will cause a deal of speculation when it becomes known we are betrothed."

"Then we won't be. We won't announce it at all. We'll merely advertise that we were wed, quietly and without fuss. I'll have the vicar read the banns this very week."

"So soon?"

"Sooner, if I can manage it."

He accompanied this declaration with a quick kiss, and the bubble of happiness, dimmed by Grace's reaction, began to revive in Marianne as he hurried her down the stairs and out of the front door.

Halfway to the old oak, whither they were headed in hopes of a little halcyon time to themselves, Alex waylaid them. "Couldn't wait to wish you happy. Jocasta told me the news."

Justin grinned as his cousin wrung his hand. "Of course she did. My flighty little sister would never think to leave me the pleasure of disclosing it to you."

"Don't matter. Guessed it must come to this sooner or later, before the two of you went up in smoke." Alex, pausing only to ask Justin's permission, gave Marianne a hug quite as suffocating as Jocasta's. He kissed her cheek into the bargain. "Must write to my mother at once. She'll be in high croak."

Marianne stared and Justin's jaw dropped.

"What? But my aunt was instrumental in keeping me from wedding Marianne in the first place. Besides arranging the match with Selina's mother."

"That's a female all over. Can't make up their minds. Told me she'd made a mistake."

"Aunt Pippa? You're jesting!"

Marianne, recalling snippets Lady Luthrie had said to her, cut in at this point. "Yes, but I don't think he is. Alex, was Lady Luthrie trying to push us together?"

"That's it. Said if Justin thought you were looking to wed elsewhere, he'd come to his senses."

Justin's hold tightened about Marianne's hand. "She was right."

"Hate to say it, but she usually is, my mother."

Marianne could not hold back the rising amusement. "She made you Justin's decoy."

Alex laughed. "Just so. And it worked."

"Why could you not have come out and said so at the outset?"

"Don't be a nodcock, coz. Had to find it out for yourself."

Justin thumped his cousin on the shoulder. "Well, and I must thank you too, Alex. You stood buff and kept me sane."

Marianne saw his cousin redden. Had she not guessed all along he had been Justin's confidant? "Have I you to thank for delivering Justin into my clutches then?"

"Nothing of the sort. Mind you, had to call him to order now and then."

"So you did. But if you will forgive me, Alex, we'll resume this discussion at a later date."

Alex cocked an eyebrow. "*De trop*, am I? I can take a hint, coz. I'll take myself off."

He shook Justin's hand once more, dropped a quick kiss on Marianne's cheek, and left them.

Resuming their leisurely progress, Marianne felt Justin take her hand again. She was charmed with the gesture, feeling all the freedom of being able to show her love by letting her fingers entwine with his, and feeling too the warmth of knowing herself beloved.

Justin was silent so long, she became a trifle concerned.

"What are you thinking?"

His hold tightened briefly, and a faint grimace came her way as he looked at her. "My stepmother's tongue betrayed me. I had not wanted to tell you of my father's words."

The light in her heart did not dim. "Well, he had reason. He was doing what he thought was the best for you."

"It is like you to be so generous, Marianne, but I can't be. He condemned me — and you too, I now learn — to purgatory, which would have lasted a lifetime had Selina not been enamoured of O'Donovan."

Remembrance of the pain sent a fleeting shadow across Marianne's happiness, but she banished it. "Don't let it trouble you. I dare say time would have done its work. You'd have found a *modus vivendi* of some kind."

"Lord knows I was trying to. I had convinced myself to think of you only as a friend. After all, I had years of practice."

"You convinced me too," Marianne said on a wry note. "And your father never showed me anything but kindness. It did not occur to me he might disapprove of a union between us."

"Which made you believe I did not care enough." He halted and turned her to him, doubt and dismay in the green eyes. "My darling, I'm sorry for that. Should I have told you? Explained why I could not offer?"

Touched to her core, Marianne blinked away a stray tear. "No, my dearest one, you did right to keep me ignorant. It would have been anguish to give you up, knowing you wanted me as I wanted you. I would have suffered for you as well as for myself."

Justin drew her gently into his arms and kissed her. Not deeply, but with tenderness that told her more than any words how this relieved him.

She did not speak again until they had reached the oak, and a wave of nostalgia went through Marianne as she recalled their many trysts in this favoured spot. Sitting with Justin's arm cosily about her, Marianne could scarcely believe all that had happened in so short a time.

"Dame Fortune has smiled kindly on us today."

Justin laughed. "And long overdue."

He signified his satisfaction with an assault that left her breathless and protesting.

"If you do that, how can I behave?"

The teasing gleam she loved appeared. "Who says I want you to?"

She struck him, but lightly. "You are quite outrageous."

"What, with you dinning proper conduct into my ears all these years? Impossible. I am a model of decorum."

"You'll be a model of a hen-pecked spouse by the time I'm done with you, dreadful creature!"

"By no means. The moment you've made your vows I'll turn into a domestic tyrant. You'll be cowed in no time."

Marianne acknowledged this ludicrous notion with a giggle, but her attention had caught. She sat up in a bang. "Justin, it's very well to talk of an immediate wedding, but how can we? You've no notion how much preparation will be needed, even for a small affair."

"Must it be such a bother? Can we not simply do the thing ourselves and —"

"No, we can't, don't be absurd! You must at least invite your immediate family, and your tenants. And the servants will wish to be present."

"Good God! I'd prefer to elope!"

Marianne set her hand on his where it rested on his knee. "You're an earl and you have a duty to your people. You can't possibly cheat them of the pleasure of partaking of your nuptials. It's an important event in your career."

He sighed, but a rueful grin came her way. "If my father could hear you, he would acknowledge himself mistaken. You're going to make the perfect countess, my love. You'll probably drive me into an early grave with your chivvying, but I dare say that's an irrelevancy."

"Not until I've presented you with an heir and a spare."

His lips quirked. "Why do you imagine I'm pressing for an early date?"

Blushing furiously, Marianne delivered another hit. "I wish you will be serious!"

Justin put his arm about her again and caught her close. "I can't be. I'm much too happy."

Such a declaration could not but gratify her and Marianne submitted to a further demonstration of his affection. When he released her, he let out a careful breath, eyeing her with some degree of anxiety.

"Marianne, my darling girl, can we not manage everything in the three weeks it must take for the banns to be read? I truly cannot wait longer for you."

Marianne met his ardent gaze and her heart turned over. Her smile was a trifle tremulous.

"Then we will manage." A thought occurred and she struck her hands together. "The village women!"

Justin began to laugh. "What in the world are you talking about, you crazy woman?"

She smiled, but caught his hand. "I was wondering how I could present an appearance appropriate to the occasion in such short order."

Consternation spread across his face. "Your bride clothes? What a clod I am! Marianne, forgive me! I should have thought of it. Pay no heed to me. Take whatever time you need."

She shook the hand she held. "No, listen. Mrs Woofferton was saying only this morning that Peggy Baker was asking for work. I will have the women fashion my gown. They did the most wonderful speedy job on the curtains for your bride's bed —"

She broke off, releasing his hand and throwing her fingers up to her mouth as recollection leapt into her mind.

Justin was at once all concern. "What ails you now, sweetheart?"

"The curtains! Justin, you can have no notion, but I must confess it now. Petherick had very little choice and time was pressing. Only when they were hung did I realise — it was utterly unconscious, I promise you, or I wouldn't have done anything so disastrously selfish."

He captured her distracted hands and held them fast. "Softly, Marianne. I haven't the least understanding of what you're saying."

She let out a series of little breaths, fighting for composure. "You see, that pattern I chose was so like one I had as a child. And the coverlet too. Almost the exact same colour."

"Was it so? I thought when I saw it how the effect was suited to your personality."

"Oh, don't say so. It was dreadful, Justin. Here was Lady Selina's chamber, and I curtained her in a cocoon expressly designed for myself. I was never more ashamed!"

She struggled, but the tears would not be suppressed, the echo of the turmoil she'd gone through over those very curtains proving too much for her control. Justin, ever resourceful, provided her with a handkerchief. Then, when she'd composed herself, kissed her damp cheeks and cuddled her close.

"It's all over now, my dear one, and it is your cocoon, your rightful place, as it should have been at the outset."

She gave a watery chuckle. "Well, at least it won't have to be done over."

He grinned and cocked an eyebrow. "Have you any more revelations, or are you done confessing your sins?"

"Well, if there are any more," she said with returning spirit, "I shan't confess them to you, you wretch."

"Excellent. As to that cocoon of yours, I can think of several interesting ways to make use of it. Would you wish me to demonstrate?"

Perceiving that her love was in no condition at this moment to be susceptible to scolds, Marianne gave herself up to a tantalising peek at just what he had in mind.

# A NOTE TO THE READER

Dear Reader,

For once in my life, a song inspired me to write a story. I became riveted one day by the words of *You Don't Know Me* as sung by the mellow tones of the King himself. For those too young to remember, I am talking about the one and only Elvis — as a forever fan, I say that with conviction.

Written in 1955 by Cindy Walker, the first version I heard was by Ray Charles. YouTube features it by Elvis, Ray Charles, Willie Nelson, Michael Bublé and a beautifully sung arrangement by Norah Jones, to name but a few artists.

The song is a heart-breaking testament to the pangs of unrequited love. The lyrics are beautiful and poignant and as the idea for a story crept into my head I couldn't stop listening to the song. So much so, I found I had learned the words by heart, though some have slipped away from me now.

The idea for the story encompassed the point of the song in that our hero thinks of our heroine only as a friend, where in truth she loves him deeply. Thus, he does not really know her. It's the poignant nag of the constant ache that makes the song so telling, and this was what I tried to recreate in the story of Justin and Marianne.

If you listen to the song, you'll find the title comes directly from a part of the lyrics:

*Afraid and shy I let my chance go by*
*The chance that you might love me too*

And Marianne does consider taking her chance, but her courage fails her.

As the story opens, I wanted to explore the exact same emotional turmoil which originates from the first verse, and this in Marianne when Justin finally arrives at the ball:

*You give your hand to me*
*And then you say hello*
*And I can hardly speak*
*My heart is beating so*

Likewise, after this painful interlude, to end that particular little scene, I wrenched poor Marianne's heart as Justin walks away with his betrothed, with a lyric taken from the final verse:

*You give your hand to me*
*And then you say goodbye*
*I watch you walk away beside the lucky guy*

The result of all this is that the story always reminds me of the song and vice versa. Of course, since this is romance, *A Chance Gone By* ends more happily for Marianne than for the unfortunate singer of *You Don't Know Me*! I leave you to judge whether the recreation is as heart-breaking as the song itself.

If you would consider leaving a review, it would be much appreciated and very helpful. Do feel free to contact me on **elizabeth@elizabethbailey.co.uk** or find me on **Facebook**, **Twitter**, **Goodreads** or my website **www.elizabethbailey.co.uk**.

Elizabeth Bailey

**Sapere Books** is an exciting new publisher of brilliant fiction and popular history.

To find out more about our latest releases and our monthly bargain books visit our website: **saperebooks.com**

Printed in Great Britain
by Amazon